BURNING ROSES

BURNING
ROSES

S. L. HUANG

T O R
D O T
C O M

A Tom Doherty Associates Book
New York

BURNING ROSES

Copyright © 2020 by S. L. Huang, LLC

A Tordotcom Book
Published by Tom Doherty Associates
120 Broadway
New York, NY 10271

www.tor.com

Tor® is a registered trademark of Macmillan Publishing Group, LLC.

The Library of Congress Cataloging-in-Publication Data is available upon request.

ISBN 978-1-250-76399-0 (hardcover)
ISBN 978-1-250-76398-3 (ebook)

Our books may be purchased in bulk for promotional, educational, or business use. Please contact your local bookseller or the Macmillan Corporate and Premium Sales Department at 1-800-221-7945, extension 5442, or by email at MacmillanSpecialMarkets@macmillan.com.

First Edition: September 2020

Printed in the United States of America

0 9 8 7 6 5 4 3 2 1

To Jesse, Mike, Emmie, and Rosie.
I love you guys even more than math,
or pie, or the math kind of pi.
I probably wouldn't help you kill
someone, but I'd help you move the body.

PART ONE

Rosa had grown old.

Or perhaps she had been old for a long time.

She leaned back in her chair, the wooden bones of the porch creaking beneath her. The setting sun flared against her eyes in a brilliant starburst, but Rosa did not close them, only squinted and let the tears wash through.

Perhaps she would be a more whole person if she cried. For what she had lost, and for what she had been.

"Flower, why so philosophical tonight?" Hou Yi came out onto the porch, her boots stomping loudly against the boards. Hou Yi did everything loudly, until she was on the hunt, when her footfalls became as quiet as the swish of one of her arrows. As quiet, and just as sure.

"What's wrong with philosophy?" Rosa said.

"It's a bad look for you." Hou Yi thumped herself down in the other chair. Like Rosa, she was a large woman, solid and muscle-bound. "You live too much in your own head. Like a tortoise squeezed up into its shell. It makes your face constipated."

The old wince ghosted through Rosa's head at the comparison to an animal. She'd struggled so hard over the years to excise that prejudice, papering over her discomfiture with firm assertions, walling even the whisper of her own intolerance away from allies or family. She'd so proudly taught her own child right, all those years ago—*grundwirgen might have animal forms, but they are the same as humans, just the same, no difference*—but no matter how she tried to pry her soul free, the same visceral disgust still curled inside her like an ugly, wizened friend: *You know what you are.*

Her bigotry had destroyed everything good in her life, and still she couldn't twist free of it.

Rosa turned her mind from the past and instead worked through Hou Yi's final phrase to unearth the meaning. She wasn't fully fluent in this tongue yet. And "constipated" wasn't a term she used regularly, fortune favor her.

"You're the one who's constipated," she said when she got it, mangling the pronunciation.

Weak comeback, but Hou Yi roared with laughter. Rosa wasn't about to give her the satisfaction of asking what she'd said by accident.

"Someday you'll learn from me and let it all push out of you. See how relaxed and open I am?" Hou Yi leaned back and fished a clay pipe out of her pocket, tipping in the tobacco in a practiced motion.

"Open, ha," said Rosa. "And where is your wife again?"

"In the moon. See? Open!"

Rosa snorted. Maybe it was an idiom, but Hou Yi had always blithely refused to explain, only laughing when Rosa asked. She'd stopped trying.

Hou Yi's striker sparked in her fingers as if she were a witch conjuring fire. She puffed at the pipe, then took a long pull and blew a perfect ring of smoke at the sunset-washed sky. "And where is *your* wife, Flower?"

"I don't have a wife," said Rosa.

"Liar," Hou Yi said amiably, and held out the pipe.

Rosa took it and closed her lips around the stem, breathing in the black tang of the tobacco smoke and refusing to think about Mei. The searing warmth unfurled inside her like she had kissed a dragon.

I kiss them and then I kill them. Another memory from which she could not escape.

A pebble hit her arm.

"Stop brooding," Hou Yi said. "I didn't scrape you off the side of the road for you to brood on my front stoop."

Rosa pulled in another deep breath from the pipe. "No, as I recall, you begged for my help."

"Begged? Hardly. It was an act of charity."

"Ha."

Too much truth to both sides. Rosa, an exiled stranger in this land, her family stripped away, and with no purpose left, nothing but her rifle; Hou Yi, who had *too much* purpose, cheerfully throwing herself and her bow in the path of every ravening monster or magical scourge until Rosa had begun to suspect she had a death wish. They fit together— tagging on to Hou Yi's obsession gave Rosa's life borrowed meaning, and Hou Yi was growing too old to succeed in such recklessness alone.

Besides, battling terrors with Hou Yi was worth something. Worth dying for, if it came to that; a small token Rosa could offer against the person she had been.

Well. As long as they only hunted dumb beasts.

The sun had dipped below the mountains now. Rosa closed her eyes, losing herself in the cooling air and the scent of tobacco.

She felt Hou Yi sit up beside her.

Rosa stiffened to alertness, her hand reaching for the smoothness of her rifle, propped within reach against her chair.

"Runner," Hou Yi said. A girl dashed through the grass toward them, her legs pumping wildly.

Rosa didn't wait. Her sling fell across the shoulder of her scarlet cloak, the weight of the rifle landing comfortably on her back. Hou Yi had bow and quiver in hand as if they had appeared from nowhere.

Rosa dumped the remaining tobacco and stamped out the ash in one move as they stepped off the porch. Thin shadows spiked like knives behind them, and their boots ate the ground in a fast jog. Rosa felt the clarity of it—diving to place herself between innocents and danger, the relieving certainty that she'd die doing something clean and right.

The girl stumbled to a stop before they reached her, her face red in the twilight and her chest heaving. "You are the Great One?" she called to Hou Yi in a piping wheeze between gulps of air. Her eyes skittered to Rosa for a moment, then away. Rosa was used to it. She was a strangeness here.

How Mei must have felt, all those years. She pushed the thought away. "Where, child?"

The girl's eyes flicked between them again, but

she wasted no time in pointing behind her and toward the south.

"The farms outside Jie Shu Kai," Hou Yi said.

"Please," said the girl. "My father—"

Hou Yi took off at a run, her strides devouring distance. Rosa was only an instant behind her. She shouted at the girl to stay behind, where it was safe, but she wasn't sure whether her words were lost in the wind.

Straight as one of Hou Yi's arrows, the two women loped in the direction the girl had pointed. The land began to push up in low hills, gentle undulations beneath their pounding tread. The sky purpled above them like an aging bruise, and before it had quite deepened all the way to black they found the fires.

Flares burst over the hills in pops of orange and gold, terrifyingly brilliant against the night. From here it was almost beautiful.

"Two of them," called Hou Yi.

Even after hunting by the woman's side for more than a year now, Rosa was still not sure how she knew from this far away.

Rosa's jaw clenched. Two. Last time, together they'd barely been able to put down one. And Hou Yi had been badly burned, a bubbling swath of blisters that had only just finished healing into a shiny scar.

Another scar for the collection, Rosa had joked, once the danger was over and the bird dead and inert.

But it was no joke. This fight truly might be their last.

So be it.

Rosa lowered her head and pushed herself faster. Ahead, dark lumps scurried over the horizon, stumbling in waving lines, racing to prop each other up. They solidified into ash-coated people as they came closer, screaming and crying, some with no more than the ruined clothes hanging off them and soot streaking their terrified faces. One older man kept trying to turn back, wailing, but his children dragged him on, their expressions dead.

Interspersed with the humans ran the odd animal, all clearly more than dumb creatures—here a snake kept rapid pace with a woman; there a tusked deer galloped by with the fear of a man in its eyes, twisting its neck around to look behind. To the side a wild horse galloped with children clinging to its back and a baby clenched carefully in its teeth by the swaddling clothes. Rosa resolutely looked past them—*The grundwirgen are fleeing just as the humans are, ignore them, ignore, focus on your purpose . . .*

Some of the escapees cried out to Hou Yi and Rosa. For help? In warning? Their cries were left behind too fast for Rosa to unravel the meaning in the words. Hou Yi didn't slow and so neither did Rosa; nothing they could do for these villagers would make any difference if they could not stop the birds.

Rosa's breath began clenching in her lungs, and her throat bucked in a spasm of coughing. Her feet stumbled, suddenly heavy, and she raised her head to find the air ahead clogged with smoke. The movement of fleeing humans, animals, and grundwirgen had become ghostly shadows. Rosa's eyes stung.

Beside her, Hou Yi paused long enough to wrap a scarf around her nose and mouth. Rosa did the same, pushing up her red muffler and binding it tight. Then she looked to Hou Yi.

The other woman scanned the haze, searching for signs Rosa had not yet learned to see. Then she pointed in quick, sweeping motions: *You, that way. I, this way.*

Rosa gave a sharp nod she wasn't sure Hou Yi could see and struck off toward where her fellow hunter had directed.

Washes of brightness came through the smoke, haze diffusing the fire into a deceitful softness. The size of the flares took her aback. Either she was near, or the bird was huge. But a glowing line against the ground had to be where the farms were set ablaze— too low, too dim for her to be near yet.

The bird was huge.

Rosa forced herself to stumble on, pushing through the smoke as if it were a physical barrier. Her hand went to her nose and mouth, clenching the muffler close. Her stinging eyes had filled with enough tears that she wasn't sure if it was salt water or ash that so blurred her vision—she closed them and drove forward.

She broke out into hell.

Fire was everywhere, dancing through broken roofs, sweeping across fields; a devouring monster neither Rosa nor Hou Yi could kill. The odd form lay unmoving across the hellscape, human or animal or grundwirgen, impossible to tell between them. Nothing but the fire moved here. The fire, and what had brought it.

The bird screamed overhead. Rosa's rifle came off her back and up out of reflex, its stock socking against her shoulder like a piece of her own body fitting into place. She brought her right hand over the top to swipe at her streaming eyes. The iron sights of the rifle snapped into focus, one behind the other, aligning with flames behind them.

Flames in the shape of a demon.

The bird spread its wings and screamed again. It towered over the scene, as big as a small cottage or bigger, its wingspan spreading twice as wide. The conflagration poured directly from its monstrous outline, engulfing the feathered silhouette and leaping to the heavens in a brilliant inferno. Half bird, and all fire.

Rosa's world reduced to the tiny front sight of her rifle, her best rifle, the one Xiao Hong had pressed into her hands that last day. Before she lost her vision again in the haze, she squeezed her finger back.

The rifle kicked her in the shoulder, but its roar was muted behind the crackling thunder of the flames. The bird screeched and reared, beating its wings down and wheeling to the side. One wing crashed through the half-burnt thatch of a house, wild, no longer responding to its owner's commands.

Rosa barely moved fast enough to save her life.

The bird reared up and pounced, its beak stabbing down exactly where she had been, fire pouring forth from its maw. Rosa dodged between burning timbers. The heat was all around, bearing down on her from every side, blistering her skin and making her heady and weak. Or was that the smoke . . . was she breathing? She couldn't tell. Her lungs curdled inside her. She tried to cough and her throat seized.

The world wavered. *If you pass out, you'll die,* she thought.

Isn't that what I deserve?

Her boot hit something. She fell. The act of

falling barely imprinted on her, as if her mind had checked out and was only waiting for the body to catch up.

Sharp grass stabbed her cheek. Eyes stared into hers, eyes blank of all life but frozen in a rictus of terror. She had tripped on a dead man.

This wasn't what *they* had deserved.

Rosa's knees wanted to bend back on themselves, but she pushed herself upright. Years of habit kept her from leaning on the rifle for help, the inane thought chasing after: *What good is the rifle if you're about to die?*

The bird had stopped screaming. Rosa tried to quiet herself to a creep—the infernal beasts had the keenest of hearing—but it was too much of a job only to keep herself ambulatory. Even in this environment, though, her hunting instincts kicked in, tracking direction, leading her to the side, around to flank, yes, that's where the wounded prey will turn.

She brought her rifle up again, so heavy now.

The bird burst forth from nowhere, from nothing, a tower of flame filling her vision. Rosa thought, *the whites of its eyes,* even though such a thing made no sense, even though the things had no eyes she'd ever been able to glimpse, and she stood strong and did not flinch as her finger squeezed back.

An avian scream, and Rosa thought, *I wounded*

it, only wounded, it's over. Her hand automatically swept back to work the bolt but no time, no time.

A dark flash of length against the fire. The arrow shaft disintegrated in immolation. Rosa did not see the arrowhead fly through.

But it must have, for this time the bird whirled in pain, its headlong charge arrested. Its wings beat at the air, the ground. The flames engulfing it dimmed and sputtered.

Rosa tried to move, but she was too slow.

The enormous, extinguishing wing came at her as if through molasses. Nowhere to duck. Nowhere to run.

The impact jarred her old bones. Then nothing.

The world still burned.

Rosa's face was against the ground, eating the dust. She tried to move. Some part of her twitched. Her rifle. Where was her rifle?

"It's you," Hou Yi said, and Rosa wanted to say, *It's I, who else would I be?* But her mouth was too slow for the thought.

"I killed you," someone else said instead.

"You killed me," Hou Yi answered.

That couldn't be right. Rosa's brain was fogged; she must be having trouble with the language, hearing the wrong words . . .

"This was you," Hou Yi continued. "You—" And here Rosa did lose the thread of meaning, catching only the word "called." Or "call." *You called me? I called you?*

"I did," the other answered.

Rosa blinked her eyes to a crack, only now realizing they had been closed. Two shapes stood before her. Hou Yi, stance firm, an arrow nocked and her bowstring drawn taut, but no sign of the strain.

And aiming at a person, a man, only a few paces before her. He too held a bow. He too held an arrow nocked, albeit loosely.

Their tableau was backlit by fire.

"What are you going to do?" Hou Yi asked.

The man lifted his bow and arrow a few inches, but did not draw tight.

"You know I . . . better . . . always," Rosa caught from Hou Yi, half the words spiraling into nonsense.

". . . better . . . ," the man responded scornfully. Then, ". . . dead."

Rosa's eyes drifted closed. When she was aware again, the man was gone, and Hou Yi's iron arms dragged her up. Rosa fell across shoulders that were as strong as an ox, and the night became blessedly cool and quiet.

* * *

Rosa woke because she was choking.

Her breath clenched in her. Her lungs seized. She woke trying to cough so hard she couldn't, and panic clawed at her—air, she needed air—

"Relax," said a voice. A strong hand on her back. Rosa gained control of her body, barely, and managed half a gasp before the coughs wracked her.

When they subsided, it was no better. Her lungs still throbbed. Her throat and eyes screamed.

Her joints ached. Her body ached. She was too old for this. "It's the smoke," Hou Yi said, entirely unnecessarily.

Rosa didn't grace that with a response. "Where are we?" she rasped instead. She was on the ground, on her cloak, the bright fabric spread like dark blood beneath her. It was still night. Late, by the deep stillness of it.

Hou Yi had started a fire. A minimal crackle of kindling, its tiny thread of smoke trailing upward harmlessly, but Rosa still wanted to wince away from it.

"We are somewhere to the southeast," Hou Yi said. Her voice had an odd quality, one Rosa couldn't pinpoint. "I am uncertain exactly where."

Rosa was too tired and sick to play this game, with Hou Yi being mysterious and Rosa refusing to ask the expected questions. *"Why?"*

"Because it got away."

At first Rosa didn't know what she meant. The man? In Hou Yi's language she needed give the statement no subject. *Got away,* she had said. Something or someone had gotten away—

"The bird," Rosa said. "You mean the other sunbird." She'd spoken in her own tongue by accident. She repeated it, the words coming with difficulty. Her brain was addled with smoke.

"Yes. It got away," Hou Yi repeated.

And Hou Yi was tracking it.

Rosa wanted to ask why, wanted to demand whether they were in any shape for such a quest, but her scratching throat revolted at the thought of trying to form the questions.

Hou Yi, for once, elaborated without being pressed. "I have to find it. It will return and wreak more damage. It's been called, and . . ." She paused. "It is my responsibility."

"It's not," Rosa said. "You don't have to." She said it more out of form than anything. Hou Yi was running from something the same way Rosa was, only Hou Yi ran by hunting the sunbirds and water monsters and other creatures that threatened the people, extending herself beyond call, beyond reason. Rosa, on the other hand . . .

Rosa had run halfway around the world and

joined a mad quest that wasn't even her own. She had no space to tell Hou Yi to stop.

Death will catch us sometime anyway. Would this be such a bad way to go?

"This is my responsibility," Hou Yi repeated. She sounded strangely remote. "But not yours. You're injured. You should return home."

Rosa pushed herself up so she was leaning on an elbow. She'd meant to get all the way to sitting, but after the effort it took to get this far, it seemed good enough. "Don't be stupid," she said. "You need me."

Hou Yi barked a laugh. "In my youth . . . but never mind. This isn't your journey. Leave. Go home. Live in my house or return to your own country; it's your decision. But this is not your path to take."

"Bull." Rosa said the word in her own language, but she was quite sure the meaning was clear. "If you're going to get yourself killed, you can at least let me do it alongside you."

Hou Yi turned her face away and touched something beneath her shirt. "You would quail away before the journey's end anyway. Go, Flower. Go find your *wife*."

The words, the image they brought up of Mei's face—they stabbed. As they were meant to. Not to mention that Hou Yi had never in their time together known Rosa to *quail*.

Hou Yi was not usually cruel.

No. Hou Yi was never cruel.

Rosa's mind spiraled back and rebuilt what she had heard and not understood. *You called them,* Hou Yi had said to the man, and he had confirmed it.

I killed you. Rosa had thought she had misheard.

Hou Yi was not usually cruel . . .

"That man is someone you knew," Rosa said. "He called the sunbirds. As . . . an act against you. Yes?"

And now Hou Yi didn't want Rosa along, was pushing her away, not because she didn't need or want aid, but because this journey would bare Hou Yi's soul. And *Rosa would see.*

Rosa wouldn't want herself, her past, so forcefully displayed either. A deep kinship thrummed through her for the violation Hou Yi must be feeling. The shame. They were meant to be able to hide from each other, together.

Hou Yi had not moved, nor responded to Rosa's query. Rosa swallowed against her swollen throat. She did not mean to do this, to know Hou Yi's secrets without having them granted to her.

But neither could she let a friend go off alone to die. Of all Rosa's faults—*and she had many, so many*—she had never been that person, and would never be.

"I had a friend," Rosa said. Her voice cracked, and she wasn't sure whether it was from the smoke or not. "I had a friend, and . . . she broke me. Then I betrayed the one who saved me from her."

Her eyes and nose burned. But if Hou Yi would be forced to reveal herself, the only thing Rosa could do was . . . the same.

If she could maintain the courage.

Hou Yi moved, finally, turning her head slightly to Rosa. "What was your friend's name?"

"Goldie. 'Little Gold,'" Rosa translated. "For her hair. Golden curls—have you seen it before?"

"I have," Hou Yi said.

"The first thing I saw was her yellow hair," Rosa said. "Through the window of a cottage. I was so cold, and so hungry. And so very lonely. My grandmother had just died, and I . . . I had been on my own." *Her icy fingers had clenched the rifle, there in the tree, outside the house where she had heard Goldie scream . . .*

"You've spoken of your grandmother before," Hou Yi said. "She taught you to hunt."

"Yes," Rosa said. "She taught me . . ."

"Still now," Abuelita's voice said at her shoulder. "Relaxed. Breathe in, breathe out, as even as you can. Like the wind caressing the petal of a flower."

Abuelita smelled of gunpowder and warm bread.

Rosa wriggled her belly against the ground and tried to relax. Inhale, exhale. Inhale . . .

"Let the rifle move with you," Abuelita said. "Up, and down. Up, and down. The same distance each time, yes? With each breath. At the bottom, your front sight kisses the target. Up, and down—kiss. Inhale, and exhale—kiss."

Rosa breathed. It was even, just as her grandmother said—she breathed, and the sight grazed the shingle that was her target. Breathe, and it happened again.

"Now, at the very bottom of your breath, squeeze your finger back. Just the tip, and so gently. Just so."

Rosa breathed, and squeezed.

The bang was so loud, even through the earmuffs Abuelita had made her wear! But the clay shingle jumped and shattered.

"I got it, Abuela! I got it, didn't I?" Without thinking, Rosa rolled out of her careful belly-down position to grin up at her grandmother's gentle face. But she kept the muzzle down out of habit, for that she had been taught long before she had ever been allowed to pull a trigger.

A proud smile wreathed Abuelita's face. "Excellent, my child! Did it frighten you?"

"No," Rosa boasted. "I want to go again!"

Her grandmother cast a quick, worried glance at the sun. "Next time. Your mother will be expecting you home."

"Can't I stay here tonight?"

"I wish, child." Her grandmother's hand touched Rosa's cheek, a feather light brush. Rosa jerked back out of reflex, before she could remember that the bruise was almost healed, and besides which, Abuela was not Mama, never never never.

"Oh. My dear," whispered her grandmother. "How I wish . . ."

But wishes never came true.

"You never speak of your mother," Hou Yi said, when Rosa ran short of words.

"No," Rosa agreed.

"I see."

Rosa had tried to turn her back on her mother when she ran, to restart her life for only herself. How ironic that the poison she'd ended up wrapping her life around had been, in the end, her mother's legacy.

No. Her prejudices were her own. She would not blame some long-ago influence that she had fled from in every other way.

"My mother was not a . . . kind woman," Rosa said instead. "I sometimes feel like she must have loved me . . . but I think I made myself forget those parts. And the grundwirgen—she was spiteful. Small comments, all the time, about how unnatural and dangerous they were. I told myself I didn't believe her, that I would be better."

"*Grundwirgen.*" Hou Yi rolled the sounds around in her mouth, badly mispronouncing them. "What a complicated word. It's your Western term for magic users, is it not?"

"Not quite," Rosa said. "It is what we call any intelligent animal. Humans who are cursed to animal form, or witches who transform themselves, or non-human creatures born with speech and intellect."

"What about gods who take the form of both beasts and humans?"

Rosa suspected, but was not certain, that the gods in this part of the world were a pantheon of extremely powerful sorcerers. But she had seen much here that she had never encountered before, so she reserved judgment. "I suppose so, yes."

"What of demons?" Hou Yi said.

"If they become animals, yes."

"What of the—" She said a word Rosa didn't know.

"I don't know. You have many more grundwirgen than we do. There is much more magic in use here."

"A very strange term," Hou Yi said. "Not very specific. The sunbirds are the children of a god, but they are a plague."

Rosa frowned. She'd insisted, when she first joined Hou Yi—"You told me they are not grundwirgen."

Hou Yi waved a careless hand. "These are dumb, yes. But others . . . I faced some in my youth who were perfectly capable of reason, but reveled in burning the countryside and countenanced nothing but their own amusement. Intelligent or not, beasts or not, such menaces must be removed."

Rosa had no good answer. "Perhaps," she said finally. She was too tired, and this was prodding old wounds from a direction she had not expected tonight. "But perhaps I am not the one to remove them."

She settled back, staring up at the stars. The fire had burned down to a pocket of glowing ash beside them. The night was so clear, the stars so bright, and Rosa had no idea where they were. It might as well have been another world.

"You need rest," Hou Yi said.

It was true. Rosa's voice was scraping into uselessness anyway. But she'd begun, and perhaps Hou Yi would take the opening of her story as the promise it was. "What's your plan? Where are we going?"

Hou Yi shifted, and sighed—a grant of permission. "We will move in the light. He is flaunting his trail at us." She paused. "His name is Feng Meng. He was my apprentice, many years ago."

Rosa didn't speak, didn't press.

"He surprised me in the woods. With a club, after he could not best me with a bow. He still would not have succeeded if the townsfolk hadn't been on his side . . . they left me when they assumed their work was done." She lowered her head slightly. "His motive was jealousy, but I am not sure he did wrong. Not then."

Rosa could understand that feeling. Whatever Hou Yi had done to swallow her in such guilt, however . . . it was not for Rosa to say the scales had been rebalanced, but Feng Meng's chosen revenge was burning a swath across the countryside. Rosa saw again the girl who had come running, gasping; saw the fleeing villagers, the burning farms; remembered the dead man's face staring into her own.

"He does wrong now," she said.

"Yes," Hou Yi answered. "And I must—*we* must stop him."

PART TWO

R osa was not sure whether she felt better or worse when she woke the next day under the wan light of a white morning sun. Every muscle had stiffened and cramped from sleeping on the ground, and every bruise from the fight the night before moaned at her when she tried to move. At least she could breathe a little more easily, though her throat and lungs felt scoured out by a pumice stone.

Hou Yi must not have come away unscathed either, but she gave no sign. She'd restarted the fire by the time Rosa woke, and had a hare spitted over it.

"Where is Feng Meng leading us?" Rosa asked. "Do you know?"

"The sunbirds come from an island," Hou Yi

said. "Just off the coast, in the sea to the south and east. They mostly keep to that place. I was wondering why they had begun venturing so far into towns and villages—usually they do not, unless they are malicious."

Maliciousness would mean grundwirgen. Rosa could only be glad she was not faced with that moral dilemma.

"The bird from last night seems to have returned in that direction. The trail of Feng Meng likewise points us on that path."

Rosa nodded. She had assumed Hou Yi had been tracking. "You think he has the sunbirds under his control?"

"Perhaps. Perhaps not. He may be studying sorcery, but it's also possible he only baited them out. The island is wild, steeped in magic, and home to many dangerous creatures. I've journeyed there once before, when I was seeking—well, it was many years ago. I think it is Feng Meng's chosen arena for some final contest with me."

"You're better than he is," Rosa said, again remembering a snippet of conversation from their standoff that she had not grasped at the time. "He never matched your skill with a bow."

"No. But I am not under the illusion this contest will be even."

Of course not. And who was to say Feng Meng would even choose archery to duel with, when he knew his former mentor could best him?

Hou Yi rose to siphon water—she paced back and forth in the heavy dew and then wrung out the sopping hem of her cloak into a waterskin she'd had hooked to her belt. While she worked, Rosa finished eating and broke camp, kicking dirt over the fire and shouldering her rifle. Hou Yi took up her bow and quiver, and they set out at a steady pace, one that would put ground behind them without scraping them dry of energy.

They didn't speak much. The sun climbed overhead, and the rolling hills began to be dotted with groves and thickets. Rosa let Hou Yi lead, but she noted the same signs the other woman followed: a trampled line in the grass, a boot print in the dirt, a broken twig by a stream. Either Feng Meng was not very good at hiding his tracks, or he wanted them to follow.

Rosa was betting on the latter.

But as the day drew on, Hou Yi seemed to curve into herself. At every new sign her mouth would flatten more, her eyes narrow, her brow tighten. By the time they paused for a late meal, her jaw might well have been carved from stone.

"She wasn't my wife," Rosa said suddenly, over

the fire. A much larger hare this time, felled by one of Hou Yi's arrows, an arrow she had then carefully retrieved and cleaned.

Hou Yi looked up from tending the flames.

"We never called each other that," Rosa continued. "But we were, to each other—I don't know if that would be thought ill of here."

"For some," Hou Yi said, and Rosa noticed her jaw had been distracted into relaxing slightly. "For some, anything different from them is scandal. If you love her, that is all that matters."

"I love her," Rosa said.

"She left?"

"I did." Rosa fixed her eyes on the crackling meat. "I left her and—our daughter. More than two years ago."

Hou Yi waited.

"I had to." The words sounded like a lie, even though they were probably the truest ones Rosa had ever said. "What I had done—it came back to destroy them. When they found out . . . they told me to go, but I'm not sure if they would have rather I . . ." She saw the coldness in Xiao Hong's face again, heard the angry demands that she turn herself in, before the girl had thrust a rifle into her hands and said *run*.

"It might have brought them more closure

if I had stayed to face the consequences of my crimes," she murmured. "Maybe that would have been best."

Maybe that would have made her at least a shadow of the woman they had thought her, instead of a monster who was also a coward.

"I became a tyrant," Hou Yi said. She wasn't looking at Rosa either, focused instead on where her hand turned the spit. "I turned from hero to villain, when my wife left. I doubt you could have done worse."

"I'm not sure these things can be compared," Rosa said. "I was a murderer. Where does that rank?"

Hou Yi digested that for a moment, then nodded slowly. "I thought it might be something like that. Your 'grundwirgen.'"

"I told myself I was doing good. I don't know when I lost my way."

Or maybe she did. The bears. And Goldie.

Or maybe it had been still earlier than that, the very first time, with the wolf. It was the one time she could not truly blame herself, not that time—but maybe there had been no coming back from such a thing, no matter how it happened.

* * *

Her grandmother had made the red cloak for her. Well, her grandmother had made her a red cloak, back when she was three or four . . . or perhaps it had been before that; perhaps Abuelita had been experimenting with the crimson dye even when Rosa was in swaddling clothes. But Rosa remembered the first hooded cloak her grandmother had enveloped her in, the bright, bright scarlet shouting her presence across the kingdom, and Rosa had taken to it so much like a second skin that she'd thrown temper tantrums when her mother tried to make her take it off.

Now Abuelita gave her a new cloak every birthday—for growing girls, she had said—and Rosa never stopped wearing them. She felt protected when she did—safe in the embrace of her grandmother. Without one of her red cloaks she was exposed, vulnerable, an eight-year-old girl like everyone else.

With one, she was invincible.

Even from her mother.

Her mother came up behind where she sat at the breakfast table and began stroking her hair. Rosa tensed. Her ear still rang from the night before, deep in her head where she almost couldn't hear it.

"Sweetheart. I'm going to give you some bread and meats to take with you when you go to your grandmother's today. She's old—she shouldn't live alone like she does. I keep telling her to move in with us."

Rosa didn't know if she liked that idea or not. On the one side, her grandmother would live with them, embracing and protecting her all day like a living version of her red cloak. On the other, she wouldn't have her grandmother's house to escape to.

She hunched into herself.

"Don't frown, Rosa. It's not becoming."

"I don't care what's becoming."

Her mother sighed. "You will. Someday you'll need to start seeking a husband, and men don't like young ladies who frown."

"Well, I don't like men."

"Now you're just being contrary," said her mother. "Someday you will grow up. Here. I'm packing up some cheese, too. I don't know how to talk to your grandmother, honestly. She's over there, old and sick and worrying us all to death—"

"She's not sick," said Rosa.

"Then why does she need that walking stick, hmm? When you're that age you're always sick. She's too stubborn, that woman. Stubborn and rude. Always has been. Do you know what she said to me back when your father first introduced me?"

"No," said Rosa.

"The very first afternoon we met, she got right in my face about politics. No manners, that woman. I told her—I was just making small talk—and all I said was that if a man chooses to become a rat then why isn't that a sure sign of his guilt? And she got all contrary about me judging rats. Rats! Like anyone abides vermin if they don't have to."

Rosa didn't answer.

"Here's the basket. Now, don't leave the path, don't talk to anyone—are you sure you can get there alone?"

Rosa didn't point out that she'd been running away to her grandmother's since she was four. Her mother insisted on pretending it didn't happen, and if Rosa reminded her then she'd also be reminded of the night before, and Rosa didn't want to disturb a Good Mood. Good Moods meant Rosa didn't get hit.

"Remember, don't speak to anyone. Don't go anywhere else. Only to your grandmother's. You promise?"

"I promise," Rosa said, and took the basket. Abuelita's bread and cured meats were tastier than her mother's, but she didn't point it out.

The woods were muted and still tonight, no wind rustling the branches. Rosa trundled down the well-worn path, the route she could have followed in her sleep. Twilight crept through the trees, graying the colors into shadow and light. Rosa was three-quarters of the way to her grandmother's when a quiet padding rustled the leaves behind her.

She spun, her red cloak whirling.

The shadows were deep enough that her eyes couldn't penetrate them. She strained her vision into the dimness.

Nothing.

"Don't be afraid," said a voice.

Rosa jumped and stumbled backward.

An enormous wolf emerged out of the bushes, his gray fur so long and thick it looked like armor. His yellow eyes focused on her, calm and intelligent.

Rosa stopped her feet and straightened her spine. She was not going to be her mother.

"Hello, sir," Rosa said to the wolf, very politely.

"Hello." The wolf stopped a few paces from her. It was so big. Rosa's heart thumped against her ribs. It's not going to eat you. It—he—he's a grundwirgen. He's not a wild animal. He won't attack.

Don't be your mother.

"I'm new to these parts," the wolf said. His voice was very deep, and with an odd overpronunciation on some words. Different mouth, Rosa supposed. A mouth so full of long, white fangs and a long, pink tongue. "I wondered if you could direct me into town."

Rosa let out a quick breath of relief before she could stop herself. Don't be your mother. He only wants directions. A gentleman.

"Go back that way," Rosa instructed him, pointing back the way she had come. "When the path opens up from the forest into a meadow, go right. There's a fence. Go down the fence . . ."

The more Rosa spoke, the more mixed up her directions felt—she was used to running fleet-footed through the forest, not describing which tree marked the fork in the path where you had to turn left because turning right brought you up to the top of the mountain which would take you two days to climb so you definitely didn't want to turn right unless you wanted to spend two days climbing a mountain . . .

The wolf had sat down on his haunches, his large, fluffy tail lying upon the leaves, and he stared at her unblinkingly as she recited. It was unnerving. Don't be your mother; grundwirgen interact differently, that's all, Rosa reminded herself, but she kept getting confused, needing to backtrack, until her descriptions muddled themselves still more.

"Thank you," the wolf said, when she faltered into silence, not sure she had been helpful at all. "You are a very kind little girl. Very kind. Where are you off to tonight?"

"My grandmother's," Rosa answered politely.

"Oh! Does she live around here?"

"Only a little ways in that direction," Rosa said, pointing.

"I did not know this part of the woods housed many people."

"Not many," Rosa said. "We have some neighbors, but they're not near. It's nicer out here than in town. More space." Town was too dirty, Rosa's grandmother always said. Dirty and loud and full of rude people. Abuelita preferred to be able to step out onto the hunting trails and breathe in the nature of the woods. "It's quieter here. No one to be nosy, my grandmother says."

The wolf dipped his head. "Thank you, little girl. You've been most helpful."

"You're welcome," Rosa said. Her chest puffed a little in pride. She was not her mother. She'd just had a perfectly polite conversation with a very nice wolf. She was a good person.

The wolf uncurled himself and turned on silent paws to pad back through the forest the way Rosa had come. She watched him disappear into the shadows. He seemed to veer off the path at the last minute, just before she lost sight of him, and Rosa's heart twisted in anxiety that she had misdirected him. She hadn't been very clear.

Hopefully he wouldn't become lost again. And if he did, hopefully he would know she hadn't done it on purpose, that she'd tried her level best to tell him the way to go, that she wasn't like her mother . . .

It was dark enough now that it was becoming hard to see. Rosa shook herself and started back on the path to her grandmother's, her feet moving a little faster. A chill wind had picked up now, and Rosa pulled the red hood of the cloak up and tugged it close, drawing the edges tight.

She was a good person. A good person. Not like her mother at all.

Rosa quickened her pace. By the time she spotted the golden windows of the cottage beckoning her in, the trees were mere black-on-black outlines around her.

The cottage door was ajar. A narrow slice of light slashed the darkness.

That was odd.

Rosa pushed at it. "Abuelita?"

"Come in, little girl," said a voice.

The voice was pitched high and feminine like it meant to be her grandmother's, but it was wrong, different, too far off and with an odd overpronunciation swallowing the edges of the words.

Rosa could have run. She should have run.

She burst into the cottage. "Abuelita!"

The wolf sat on the floor by the fire. He looked up at her with those yellow eyes and licked scarlet off his fangs. Then he leapt.

He was so fast. Rosa threw the basket at his face and

sprinted—but not back out, she dashed sideways, toward the door to her grandmother's bedroom. She hardly knew what she was doing. "Abuelita!" she screamed, the cry tearing out incoherent. "Abuelita!"

The wolf landed on silent paws and his haunches bunched as he leapt at her again, a growl in his throat, that gray fur rising on his back in a spiky peak.

Rosa couldn't make it to the far wall. She skidded around against the hearth. A pot bubbled there, unwatched—the dinner her abuelita had been making. The fire tongs had fallen, dropped, halfway in the embers. Rosa grabbed the end, ignoring the searing pain in her hands, and whipped around, the red cloak blossoming around her. She brandished the tongs—the other end was cherry-hot, glowing and warping the air. "Get away from us!" she shrieked. "Get away!"

The wolf snapped at her and then lurched back, snarling, the smell of singed fur sharp in the small space. Rosa scrambled backward against the wall—the tongs were cooling, the other end dimming to a grayish orange. She groped a hand out against the wood, looking for another weapon, for anything to defend herself with.

The wall was wet with droplets of red.

Rosa's hands stung, pain shooting up her arms as her blistered fingers slipped. The wolf paced close, his *monstrous coat of fur standing up so tall on his back that it made his silhouette into a horrifying demon. His lips pulled back from a white-and-red mouth, his yellow eyes fixed on her. Near enough that her face felt the hot reek of his breath.*

The tongs were almost cool.

Her grandmother's hunting rifle. It was in the chest in the corner—if Rosa could get there. She backed toward it as fast as she dared, waving the tongs wildly before her. The wolf waited, his tail twitching from side to side, waiting for her weapon to stop being a weapon so he could finish his meal.

"Why are you doing this?" Rosa wasn't sure why she said it. Or how. Her mouth barely managed the shape of words.

"Wild animals have to eat," responded the grundwirgen, licking his muzzle.

"But you're not a wild animal! You're not—you're not!" The grundwirgen were just like people, just like people, just like—

"How we are treated is what we become. You will learn, little girl. When you humans want me to be feral so badly, it is the easiest thing in the world to satisfy you." The edges of his mouth drew back farther. Whether he meant it as a terrifying smile or a threat didn't matter. His teeth were enormous, curved, and very sharp.

The backs of Rosa's knees hit the chest, and she almost fell. She brandished one hand behind her, seeking the hasps, pushing at the top.

"You won't be able to hide from me in there, little girl. A dog like me can chew through leather, didn't you know?"

Rosa plunged her arm in, and her fingers closed around the polished wood of the gun.

Time slowed as she heaved it out in one huge move, the tongs clattering to the floor as she brought the barrel around and caught it against her other hand. It was so big, and heavy; she'd never fired it without either her grandmother's help or being braced on the ground. She was completely off balance and didn't even look at the sights, her finger tightening the moment the muzzle crossed the monstrous gray form of the wolf.

He had time to bridle at the sight of the rifle, claws skidding on the floor as he attempted to arch back and spin away, but the gun fired with an earth-shattering roar, mule-kicking Rosa in the shoulder, and he twisted and collapsed with a whine very much like a puppy's.

He tried to get up again, scrabbling for the still-open door, for the freedom of the night, blood pouring thick and black from the hole torn in his hide. But Rosa worked the lever on the rifle and fired again, and again, and again and again until the trigger clicked down on nothing.

The final few slugs had only impacted a corpse. The wolf lay in the middle of her grandmother's living room, a massive and deformed mess of fur and blood.

Rosa's shoes bumped against it. She'd been moving forward as she fired.

Her throat was raw. She'd been screaming, too.

Her breath heaved in her chest, and she was shaking, her grip so tight on her grandmother's rifle she couldn't pry it loose, and what had just happened, and where was her grandmother?

Her face clogged, her eyes blurring. Heaving sobs took her, collapsed her. She clung to the rifle. "Abuelita!" she cried. "Abuelita . . ."

She backed up until she hit the wall again. Smeared an arm across her face until the sleeve of the red cloak was sopping with wet.

She didn't have the strength to stand anymore. Instead she crawled, still dragging the rifle with her like it was a security blanket, the empty rifle, and she should have found more cartridges for it, they were in the trunk, too, but she couldn't turn and go back now, and where was her grandmother where was her grandmother—

The door to the bedroom was open. Rosa crawled inside and found her.

* * *

"I fled then," Rosa said as she and Hou Yi hiked into the late afternoon sun. The terrain had grown more rocky now, slowing their pace and making the tracking harder, but Feng Meng was still making no attempts to hide himself. Baiting them.

"How old were you?" Hou Yi asked.

"Eight years old. I took my grandmother's rifle and ran. I hugged it at night while I lay on the ground and cried, and I repeated to myself that my mother had been right about the grundwirgen until the tears stopped."

She spoke very evenly.

Hou Yi pondered. Then she said, "Killing. It changes a person."

"Yes," Rosa said.

They walked in silence for a few minutes.

"When I stopped crying, I decided it was a crusade," Rosa said. "Or maybe deciding that is why I stopped crying. I was no longer the girl; I was the rifle. I would be an angel of justice and vengeance. I would hunt."

"You wanted to save people."

"I think saving people was the excuse. I wanted to feel powerful. I wanted to feel like nothing could ever hurt me again."

She had wanted to kill.

"I almost failed from the beginning," Rosa

continued. If only she had. *What might have been different?* No, she would never undo it, no matter what she had done, because what would have become of Mei then? She would never undo it. But she could regret, and mourn, and condemn. "I was starving to death. Sick. Out of ammunition. And the grundwirgen I so wanted to bring to justice, the ones I imagined devouring families every night while I slept . . . I could not find them. Grundwirgen are not so common in the West."

"Because of your people's prejudice?"

"I don't know," Rosa answered. "That's not supposed to be. We were always taught, everyone always says, grundwirgen are the same as people. But my mother was not alone in her sentiments."

"In the West do you harbor such feelings against any use of sorcery?"

The "you" stung, even if it applied. *Not all of us,* Rosa wanted to defend, but how could she say so, when she wasn't even in that number?

"Magic is not so—everyday, for us," she said with an effort. "I'm not sure what the answer would be." Here, Rosa had seen flying children's toys, and human women with horns, and people conjuring water by the side of the road, all as if it was of little import. Certain things still shocked and amazed here, but she was at a loss to figure out where that line was in the minds of the common folk.

Hou Yi stopped walking. Rosa thought for a moment she had lost the trail, but then she said, "Flower. You need not tell this story, if you don't wish to revisit this memories. It is all right."

Rosa squinted into the sun. Its brightness made her eyes prickle with tears.

"I haven't yet told you about Goldie."

Light. Square windows of light through the pitch-black forest, wavering in Rosa's vision. A house.

Hunger and cold and weakness had so hollowed her out that she plunged toward it with an animalistic need, groping through the heavy brush.

Maybe they would give her something to eat. Maybe they would let her lie inside their door. Maybe she could curl against the wall outside next to the chimney and the heat from the fire would bleed through the wood and they wouldn't see her there to chase her off with a hoe until morning.

The outline of the cottage wept and wobbled, now its own sturdy shape, now the welcoming silhouette of Abuela's house, promising warmth, and food, and snug protection from the least harm. All she had to do was reach it.

Rosa fetched up against a tree, panting. Walking was . . . so much work.

Someone inside the house screamed.

Fire flooded Rosa's veins, fountaining in her, sparking her nerve endings to life. Something crashed inside the cottage.

She couldn't see inside from here. She needed a vantage point.

She ran, heaving and coughing but ignoring it. There, a low fork in a tree, not twenty yards away from the window. She scrambled up, one hand staying squeezed around the rifle as if fused to it.

One cartridge. She had one cartridge left.

The bark scratched at her palm, scraped through her ragged clothes and the skin that stretched empty over her bones. Rosa made herself steady on the branch and pushed her back against the hardness of the trunk, drawing her feet up to brace against the branches on either side and anchor herself solid. The rifle came up in her hands, her elbows sturdy against her knees as her grandmother had taught her.

A scream echoed through the woods again; at the same time Rosa registered a pretty blond girl through the window, her own age, opening her mouth to cry out.

And advancing on her—bears.

Three of them.

Three bears, and Rosa only had one cartridge left.

The bears didn't seem to be in any hurry. The initial, reflexive question she'd always been taught to ask—animals or grundwirgen?—was immediately answered by the fact that the two huge ones sat in chairs in the girl's cottage. Rosa's jaw clenched. Had they devoured her parents already, taken their places to terrify her?

The girl was backed up against the chimney. The smaller bear waddled on its hind legs, toward her and away, its mouth moving in what had to be human speech, but Rosa was too far away to hear it.

The blond girl screwed up her face and screamed again.

Abuelita. *Had she screamed, in her cottage? Rosa had not come. No one had.*

But three grundwirgen, and one cartridge! If she shot one, maybe the other two would run? Or would they take the girl hostage? Be so enraged they'd rip her to shreds?

The small bear—well, smaller than the other two—was waving its paws at the girl, its claws curved and sharp. Taunting her. It waddled back toward its friends, then back toward her.

Rosa didn't have much time. Unless they were full from the girl's parents, the bears might stop taunting and start eating anytime.

The small bear went back and forth again—talking to the other two, turning back to the girl.

Wait.

Rosa moved before she had thought it all the way through. If she scrambled to the other side of the tree—branch cracking, bark scraping, her boots slipped and she almost fell, no, catch on the trunk, pull over—yes! The two seated bears lined up in her sights perfectly, the outlines of their snouted heads overlapping.

Now all she needed to do was wait for the third bear to wander back.

Would one cartridge be powerful enough? It would fly through the first animal, surely. But three?

She'd have to aim for their heads, not the huge furred slabs of bone and muscle that were their bodies. Three heads, one shot.

She wanted to cry. It was too unlikely. But she forced the thought away, forced herself to slow her breathing. Rested her elbow on her knee, the rifle on her palm, the stock snugged into her shoulder where it braced against the tree.

Just as her grandmother had taught her.

Breathe in, out.

In, out.

The pad of her finger teased the trigger, ever so slightly.

She would rescue this girl. If she did nothing else in her life, she would save this girl.

In, out. In . . . out . . .

The small bear roared at the girl again, its teeth stabbing at her, and she shrank back, but Rosa narrowed her focus, front sight, steady . . .

The small bear waddled back toward its fellows—

In, out, and as her targets crossed each other . . .

. . . squeeze.

The roar of the rifle ripped the night in half. The recoil slammed Rosa's bony shoulder against the tree, and the rifle suddenly felt heavy, so heavy she almost let it tumble from her fingers before tightening them. She gulped in a ragged breath of frigid air and forced her exhausted eyes to raise back to the window.

The bears were down, their bulk collapsed in furred mountains. The small one still moved.

The blond girl stared at them, paralyzed. She wasn't running. Why wouldn't she run? She had to run!

Rosa half slid, half fell down the tree. Whatever frisson of necessity had kept her going, it was bleeding out of her, and she stumbled and wove toward the cottage. Get the girl out. Then she could fall.

Her boots tripped over themselves as she burst in the door. The two large bears were dead, their faces gone. Lumps of fur and claw with blood for faces, no teeth left—no teeth left—the thought made Rosa want to giggle, suddenly and inexplicably and inappropriately.

The small bear was on the ground, but it twitched, still alive. Blood marked the floorboards beneath it. Rosa's eyes raked its fur but couldn't find the wound. It had been the last one in line—her bullet must have been tumbling so slowly by then.

The bear turned its furred face toward her, its lips peeling back from jagged incisors. For half a moment Rosa thought the grimace was a threat until the animal bleated, "Why?" and she realized it was only trying to speak.

"When you try to eat people," Rosa said—and her voice was shaking, why was it shaking?—she was shaking. "There are consequences."

"We weren't . . ." mumbled the bear. Its voice was higher than she would have expected.

"I'm vengeance," Rosa said. "I'm justice." The world was waving in front of her eyes, dripping in squiggles. She tried to find the other girl with her eyes, and couldn't.

The bear whined, a disturbingly human sound. "You don't under—she was—"

It stopped. Something thumped. The small bear's mouth yawned slack, its beady black eyes now turned to the wall.

Rosa tried to look up, to focus. The blond girl stood over the bear with what looked like a slightly misshapen adz head, hewn of rough stone. It was bloody.

"Thank you," she said, and her lip trembled. "They attacked me. They were about to do—unspeakable things. Thank you so much."

Something felt wrong, but Rosa couldn't . . .

"You saved my life," the girl said, her eyes lowered and timid.

Where had the rifle gone? Oh, Rosa was still holding it.

"Are you okay?" The meek gratitude had straightened out of the girl's face to be replaced with frank curiosity. A moment later it was back, like a mask. "Are you all right? They broke in, they—you saved me."

Rosa felt like sitting down. The floor came up to meet her, much too close. Once she was sitting, it didn't seem reasonable not to lie down, not when she was so near to the floor like this.

She lay and stared at the ceiling. The light was eclipsed by a small pale face. Lighting the girl from behind the way it did, the illumination in the cottage turned the tumble of blond curls into a glowing halo.

"Angel," Rosa muttered.

"What? No. Not that." The girl laughed. The frightened weakness was gone again. "Call me Goldie. And *you're my avenging angel today." She looked over her shoulder. "Look, uh—there are beds here, and there's some pretty good porridge. And I'm sure there's probably some other food—you look like a skeleton." She poked Rosa's shoulder and wrinkled her nose. "Whatever's wrong, we'll get you better."*

It drifted across Rosa's mind that the girl's words didn't fit together quite right for someone talking about her own cottage, but the thought was gone before she could grasp at it, a wisp in the wind. She stared up at nothing, and at the edges of her eyes loomed the two great chairs where the bigger bears had been seated, sitting like humans before she killed them.

The chairs were really quite large and sturdy for human ones. Goldie's parents must have been very heavy.

Maybe that was why the bears had wanted to eat them.

"I wasn't stupid," Rosa said. "I knew—of course I knew it wasn't her cottage. I figured later that she'd probably been stealing from them, and they surprised her, and she screamed. But I justified it to myself. Told myself they were probably going to eat her anyway, and nobody deserved that. After all, they were *bears*."

The sky had grayed to night again, this one gauzed with clouds but warm. By mutual silent consent they had lit no fire this time, bedding down on their cloaks. Feng Meng might assume they followed him, but why make it easy for him?

"Besides," Rosa continued softly, "Goldie had saved my life. I was nearly dead with fever in that house, and she got me out of there and back to where she had water and blankets. More importantly, after that . . . she became my friend. She shared her food with me, taught me to pick pockets and run scams, and once I shared my quest to hunt evil grundwirgen, she threw herself into finding them for me. She did it with such zeal, as if it were a game, and I—perhaps I thought she was not serious enough about something that had become tantamount to my religion, but it did not worry me. She was so slick, so sure of herself. And I . . . I idolized her. I would have done anything she asked of me."

"We are always blind to the faults of those we love," Hou Yi said.

"Feng Meng?" Rosa asked.

Hou Yi nodded.

Rosa felt no surprise. "He was more than your apprentice, wasn't he?"

"He was like a son." Hou Yi's expression wasn't visible in the dark. "Not only my son. My—legacy. Like your grandmother taught you . . . did you teach your daughter your skill with the rifle?"

"I taught Mei." *Reaching across to adjust her elbow, her face dipped behind the sights, so pale and serious and achingly beautiful. That sparking tingle as they touched, like firecrackers under Rosa's skin.* She gently closed the lid on the memory. "Mei taught Xiao Hong."

They both had, to be truthful, but Rosa could not have been prouder of stepping back and watching Mei repeat those same precious words to a tiny, exuberant, *perfect* child, the same words Abuelita had given Rosa and Rosa had given Mei and now Mei was passing on in turn, in one long unbroken thread of love.

She felt a deep stab of grief for Hou Yi as if it were her own.

"You understand then," Hou Yi said. "Everything I was, everything I knew, I wanted to give to him. I felt unbridled joy at his successes. If he had surpassed me, it would have been cause for celebration, but it also didn't matter that he did not, only that we kept learning, together."

"But he didn't feel the same."

Hou Yi's silhouette was still in the night, and Rosa was not sure she had heard. But then her shape crumpled, her hands coming up to her face. "Where did I go wrong?" she whispered.

PART
THREE

They started early the next morning. The air was cooler today, and the breeze carried a tang of salt. They were nearing the sea.

Hou Yi picked up the thread from the evening before, as if it had been left trailing on the ground in the dark. "You must doubt," she said, after they had begun their steady hike. "You must wonder if I'll be too soft to stop him, when the time comes. I don't know myself."

Rosa had wondered. She had not yet known how to broach the question. She'd determined to stand with Hou Yi, to be her second, but . . . what would that mean?

"It's one reason I didn't want your companionship, and also a reason I do," Hou Yi said. "Because you might see me fail. But I might need you to prevent it."

This was Rosa's gravest concern. "Do you plan to . . ." She wet her lips. "What do you plan to do?"

"I don't know."

Rosa had never killed someone in human form, though she knew that distinction was only in her mind. More importantly, she had not killed anyone at all since that day long ago when she had betrayed the person she had loved more than anyone in the world. *"You saved me, you saved me," he babbled, groveling at her feet as a toad hopped away, and then she put her rifle to his skull and pulled the trigger.*

"I made a promise," Rosa said. "It's why I . . . stopped. A long time ago."

"I would not ask you to break such a promise. We shall see what we shall see." Hou Yi coughed. "Perhaps it is a foolish hope, but I still wonder . . . if I can reason with him. If I can meet him and reach out to him and tell him to come home."

Her voice was laced with pain. Rosa did not think it very likely, but she also knew she would have hoped the same in Hou Yi's place, no matter how slim the chance.

"I'd done such terrible things," Hou Yi continued, almost as if to herself. "That day Feng Meng surprised me in the woods. I had . . . my position at the time was a very high one, because of the deeds I had accomplished protecting people, and I . . . after I lost my wife, I wanted them all to feel the same pain. I thought, *they only have this world because I saved it,* and yet they still clamored for more from me, need, need, need, want, want, want—and I was numb to all but my misery. I made them one with my grief in every way I could."

Rosa could offer no advice, not when it came to escaping that long shadow of guilt, the one whispering that a bad death was no less than they had earned.

It might even be true.

"Feng Meng had turned from me long before then," Hou Yi said. "His act was not one meant to protect the people from his former mentor who had gone too far. In fact, he was the reason . . . but I would still willingly forget it all, if he would. As I might hope the people I wronged may do for me, someday, if they can."

Rosa would have hoped such a thing as well, but most of the people she had wronged were dead, save two. The two who mattered to her more than anything.

"Tell me about your wife, Flower," Hou Yi said, as if she had read Rosa's thoughts. "Your Mei. I hope you and she have a happier ending than mine."

Their ending had already been written; Rosa was just waiting for the time to run out.

But she did not say that aloud.

The first time Rosa saw Mei was in a garden.

Rosa had come here to hunt. She'd perched in a blind where she could see over the wall, into this castle where rumor held that a fearsome beast dwelled, a onetime prince who had been cursed from humanity long ago. Holding a princess captive to his depraved needs.

And instead of the Beast, she had seen Mei.

Mei had been so young. Barely more than a girl, and not a princess at all, Rosa found out later—only an unlucky child who had been sold to someone still too royal for the laws to apply to him. She wore her hair loose, and it fell in thick, black waves past her waist. Her skin was so pale that the contrast was striking, black and white, coal and ivory.

Rosa's sights dipped, and she stopped breathing.

Mei was making a slow circuit of the garden. She reached out and touched one of the roses, a late red bloom. Almost as if she was sorry for it.

The Beast came out.

Rosa had expected a lumbering, ugly thing, clumsy and misshapen. Instead, he was graceful. He moved like a giant cat, his bulk becoming light in his bound across the garden, and he wore the magnificent ermine-trimmed cape of the prince he had been. He whirled through the roses and approached Mei.

Such an overwhelming hate engulfed Rosa that she almost choked on it. She'd never in her life felt such a thing. Her hands went white-knuckled on the rifle.

But then Mei had reached out to the Beast and touched him, gently, with affection. She twisted the red rose from the bush and held it out. The Beast took it and cradled it to his breast, and he bowed his head to her.

Rosa's hands trembled and hesitated. For the first time, she did not know what to do.

And so, after she'd watched the Beast leave the next day to prowl or hunt or whatever he left his remote castle to do, Rosa found herself climbing down from the blind and over the wall and into the garden.

Her step on the gravel made barely a sound. But the roses were so quiet that Mei turned immediately.

Rosa had never felt so rough or ungainly. Goldie had started calling her "my big brute" of late—affectionately, Rosa insisted it was affectionate, and it was true, wasn't it?—but now she felt every inch of the description in a way that she wished she didn't.

Mei started when she saw another person inside the walls with her. She stared at Rosa. Her breath quickened.

"Hello," Rosa said, absurdly. "I saw you over the—I'm not going to hurt you." Mei's eyes had flicked to the rifle.

"I don't think you will," Mei said, as if this was surprising to her. "Who are you?"

"I'm—nobody. I didn't—my name is Rosa." Why was she suddenly stumbling over her tongue?

But Mei smiled, and it was like warmth coming after a long winter. "Rosa," she said. "They are your kinsmen, then." And she gestured to the flowers.

Later Rosa thought that was the moment she was gone. Even when Mei refused to leave with her, to let herself be rescued, even when she insisted the castle was her home, a home she had been sold to—sold to!—seven years before.

Even when she would not let Rosa kill the Beast and set her free.

It was the subject of their first real quarrel, after they'd been stealing kisses in the woods for months, after Goldie had begun to demand where Rosa kept haring off to and Mei's increasing remoteness had begun to shorten the Beast's temper even more than usual.

"I don't understand you," Rosa had snapped that midwinter day, when Mei had yet again stated that she could not leave, even for a few days, even to see the mountains or the city or people or some place that was not the walled garden and its iron-fisted master. "I don't understand how you can let him do this to you! He's kept you his prisoner—how can you want to stay?"

"I don't—I don't know," Mei said. She pinched her hands together, the way she did when she was nervous or upset. The way she did when they came back late and she was afraid the Beast might suspect she had snuck out, the way that usually made Rosa's hands itch for her rifle. "He's not as strong as you think he is. If I leave him alone here . . . Rosa, he needs me. He says he'll die without me."

"Bull," Rosa said. "And even if he would, so what? You don't owe him anything!"

"It's been just the two of us here, for so many years," Mei said. "I've—I care for him. It's hard . . ."

"You never saw anyone else because he kept you here!" Rosa shouted. She knew she was losing her temper, but it seemed appropriate. "He's brainwashed you. He's manipulating you. Whatever good feelings you have for him, they aren't real."

"Of course they're real." Mei drew herself up, and her voice went colder in a way Rosa hadn't yet heard from her. "And they're mine. I know what he has done. I'm not so naive as you seem to want me to be."

Rosa drew back, stung. "Reading books is not the same as—"

"So, what, then? I should bow to the whims of the first person who drops into my garden?" Mei said. "Instead of honoring what I feel myself? Is that what you would require of me, Rosa?"

"No! I'm trying to tell you what's best for—" Rosa cut herself off. The two of them stared at each other.

"I'm not your child," Mei said into the silence. "Nor your pet, nor some flower to be tended. And perhaps you should look to the poison in your own life before you judge mine."

Rosa turned away and wrapped her red cloak around herself more tightly. "You haven't met her. You have the wrong impression."

"Then why do you lie to her every time you come here?" Mei asked. "Why do you always make excuses for what she says to you? At least I know how ill I've been used, even if I can't wish away how close I've grown to him despite it." She drew back, resettling herself and staring up at the white winter sky. "I can't tell you to turn away. She's your family. Family is difficult. I understand."

"She's my friend," Rosa said stoutly, too loudly. "She's been there for me when no one else in the world, when—I'm not going to turn my back on her. So she's not perfect. Nobody is."

They stood in that unhappy place together, there in the snow. Then Mei turned to go back to the castle, but her step paused, her head bent so Rosa only half saw her face through a curtain of ebony hair.

"Give me time," she said, so softly Rosa almost didn't hear.

* * *

Rosa trailed off in the telling, her voice rasping to silence.

Hou Yi digested the tale for a moment. Then she said, "She came from this land, didn't she? I understand now."

Rosa nodded. "Long ago. The Beast who had trapped her—he had been cursed to that form by a witch for his selfishness and temper, and only the love of a woman would break the enchantment. His way of forcing that love was to buy a foreign bride and keep her imprisoned until she forgot the rest of the world." Rosa's mouth twisted. "Mei's father sold her to pay his own debts. She was only a child."

Hou Yi made an angry sound in her throat.

"After so many years, I know she no longer considered this place her home," Rosa continued. "Not a surprise, is it? But I suppose I came here because . . . I had to run somewhere. And it makes me feel closer to her than I am."

"Or you wish to keep tearing your pain open anew," Hou Yi said.

Rosa was thrown. "What? I'm not—"

Hou Yi's hand thrust out, blocking Rosa's path.

Rosa was about to protest, but her friend's attention had flown elsewhere, her bow unslinging in the space of a breath with an arrow slipping onto the string. She flashed Rosa an impish smile and said, "Look. Lunch."

Rosa looked. A hare, one of the largest hares Rosa had ever seen, had come unnoticed not six strides from them. It sat on its haunches gazing in their direction, and seemed oddly unafraid of them, for a hare . . .

Hou Yi's bow whipped up.

The realization collided in Rosa's head with the speed of a rifle blast, but even that was too slow. She tried to push Hou Yi's arm aside, but the woman had already loosed, sending an arrow directly at the heart of the grundwirgen hare.

But somehow, impossibly, between the twang of the bowstring and the arrow's near-instantaneous flight, the hare stepped aside. Slowly, calmly, as if it had all eternity to scoot its haunches a few hand-spans over. The arrow whistled through where it had just been, skimming harmlessly into the grass behind.

Hou Yi sucked in a breath and then said a word Rosa didn't know, but it sounded like a curse.

The two of them stared at the hare. The hare stared back.

Hou Yi had nocked another arrow—so fast and fluidly Rosa hadn't seen—but she kept her bow only half raised. Rosa touched her rifle, lightly, the polished wood of the stock reassuring on her fingertips, but did not unsling it. Yet.

"Do you think—Feng Meng?" Rosa asked. She wasn't sure whether she meant the hare itself might be the man transformed, or whether it was more likely the beast had been sent to do his bidding somehow.

"Unclear," Hou Yi answered. She sounded unnerved.

The wind rustled through the surrounding vegetation. The hare's nose twitched lightly, only emphasizing its unnatural stillness.

"Who are you?" Hou Yi called. "What do you want from us?"

The hare sat silent. Nose twitching.

Rosa repeated an approximation of the same question in her own language, just in case—not that she expected it to have any result here. The hare didn't seem to hear either of them.

"What do we do?" Rosa said.

Hou Yi took a moment to think. "We walk."

But she kept her arrow nocked as she led a wide berth around the animal. Rosa followed, sidestepping so the creature never left her vision.

As soon as they were past, the hare hopped twice, following.

They stopped. It stopped, too. Hou Yi took one more experimental step. The hare scooted forward again, just once.

The light breeze seemed suddenly chilling.

Every cautious step forward they took, the hare matched exactly. Rosa and Hou Yi eventually resumed their steady pace, but now always with an eye behind them. The hare never approached any closer, always keeping itself the same six strides distant.

For a luncheon, they dug roots beside a stream, unwilling to hunt the hare's kin in front of its watchful eyes. Hou Yi was visibly disturbed, shifting where she'd crouched to rest, her hand always hovering near her bow.

"Why doesn't it speak?" she murmured.

Rosa couldn't help but suspect it was waiting for them to turn their backs. But she wasn't sure if it was a true apprehension or her old biases, so kept her own counsel.

"Perhaps it can't," she said instead. She tried a mangled greeting from every people she could remember encountering, but with a similar lack of results. "Do you speak anything else?"

Hou Yi grunted and tried a dialect Rosa didn't know. "The language of my hometown," she added, by way of explanation.

It still boggled Rosa that this land had so many tongues, all different village by village, with sometimes only the trade language in common—and sometimes not even that. She'd offered to teach Hou Yi some of her own speech, but Hou Yi had cheerfully refused.

"Your Western tongues are so ugly," she'd said. "And they insist on calling me a man."

"No, that's not true," Rosa had protested. "Just tell people you're a woman, and they'll use the right words for you."

"*Tell* them? Every time? That seems so very tiring," Hou Yi had answered, and that had been the end of the discussion. Hou Yi *had* gamely tried to master Rosa's name, but had eventually declared it impossible to say, settling instead on a Rosa-approved translation.

"Keep on with your tale," Hou Yi said as they began their hike again, wading across the creek. The hare made seemingly impossible leaps between stones to cross the water, its hops effortless. "I need a distraction from this hellbeast. Besides, you have me in suspense."

Rosa did not like to talk of something so personal with such large listening ears nearby, even though her story would be of no import to anyone here. But that, too, felt like her old prejudice pushing at her, and she shoved back against it.

She did try to keep her voice low, however. "I think I knew it could not end well. We both did." She gave the hare a sidelong glance, but it made no outward change, and she forced herself on. "We were headed for a precipice, inevitably, even as we dug our heels in against it as long as we could."

"And where have you been?" Goldie demanded. "I was getting worried. You shouldn't scare me like that." She lounged on a velvet-draped chair as if it were a throne, pouting prettily. Puss was beside her, as always these days, and he looked up from buffing his claws to throw Rosa a look that perfectly expressed his boredom with her.

I have no use for cats anyway, she thought. Why did Goldie keep him around? She'd always chased rumors of the grundwirgen with the same fervor as Rosa, glorying in the planning of their next target, and now suddenly a cat was off-limits? Goldie claimed she liked Puss's scamming skills, but Rosa had vowed to herself never to turn her back on him—or have her rifle far from hand.

She tried to ignore the squirming question in her

gut that asked why Goldie delighted so much in Rosa's hunting, if she did not truly believe it was the only possible justice.

"You better not be making messes without me, Red," Goldie said, interrupting Rosa's uncomfortable train of thought. "If I have to clean up after you without getting any of the fun parts, I'm going to be m-a-a-ad."

"When have you ever had to clean up after me?" Rosa said.

Goldie stretched. "Puss and I have a party tomorrow night. You're welcome to come, but only if you're not going to poop all over it. You're always in a mood these days."

"Are you working it?" Rosa asked.

"Of course." Goldie rolled her very blue eyes. She'd grown up to be the type of woman every man stared at, tall and willowy and all slender curves, and that hair of spun-gold curls. And she used her looks to every advantage. "I hear there will be an earl there. Maybe he'll take pity on a poor baron's daughter whose father has gotten himself into a wee spot of trouble."

Rosa could tell Goldie wanted her to ask the rest of the planned game. Feeling contrary, she refrained. "I'll pass."

"What is with you?" Goldie asked crossly. "You never want to do anything fun anymore."

"She has a lover," Puss said, in his bored cat hiss.

Goldie sat bolt upright, as if she'd been shocked into straightness. "Red! How could you?"

Rosa turned away and busied herself with shucking her cloak and properly stowing her rifle. Her immediate defensiveness wanted to demand why Goldie should care one way or the other. But somehow she'd known Goldie would care. She'd known every time she went to see Mei and lied about it.

"What do you mean, how could I?" she settled on saying. "You jump through more beds than I can count."

"Yes, but I don't love *any* of them." Goldie pushed her bottom lip out in a pout. "Well, get rid of her. It's just supposed to be you and me. Can't have some floozy hanging around."

Rosa very much wanted to give Puss a pointed look then, but didn't.

"Lovers just interfere," Goldie added, with finality, as if that settled matters and it was time to change subjects. "How's the dragon coming?"

She has a name, Rosa didn't say.

As relieved as she was to escape interrogation about Mei, Rosa would have chosen any change in topic but this. She didn't know why this hunt had started to disturb her so. Of all the grundwirgen she'd brought justice to, Bistherne warranted it more than any—she had been such a terror to the countryside that there was a great reward for her death.

And she'd been the first Rosa had failed to kill.

Bistherne had been amused by this. And more amused by Rosa's second try, and third.

"You're more interesting than most humans," she had said. "Usually I eat the ones who come to slay me. It seems only fair. But I think I'll let you try again."

By rights Rosa should have wanted to kill her more than any other. It was an affront to her pride.

"Do you know what they call me?" she'd demanded of Bistherne once, and the great serpentine creature had only laughed a great serpentine laugh, smoke puffing out of her nostrils.

"What do they call you, little one? Enlighten me."

Rosa hated being condescended to. "I'll be back to show you."

But the dragon had only laughed again, and the months had passed, and Rosa had made every excuse to herself not to return.

It was easy, when Mei didn't want her to.

"She's toying with me," she had complained to Mei. "But she's interesting. I almost don't want to see her go. Why should I care if she's wreaking havoc among the King's Men? I hate the king."

"So don't kill her," Mei said. "If you don't want to kill her, don't."

"It's who I am," Rosa said.

"It doesn't have to be."

Mei had never asked her to stop hunting, but Rosa knew.

"I suppose it had started to feel pointless anyway," Rosa said to Hou Yi. "I was changing. She changed me."

"Love can do that," Hou Yi agreed.

"Hunting had been my all. And every kill, Goldie egged me on, toasted me in stolen wine. It had become my reason for living. Until it wasn't any-more, and I started to see . . . I started to look at myself with new eyes."

With Mei's eyes.

She'd stood there one day, Goldie laughing at the bear they had cornered and killed, and as he lay dying, he turned back into a man, his human eyes filled with fear. "No mercy. They all said you . . . no mercy," he choked, his eyes rolling first over Goldie's pale form and then Rosa's dark one. "The ice queen . . . Ice White and Blood Red . . ."

Blood Red, they all called her, Rosa knew. Those whispers in the dark, the men and grundwirgen who *rightfully feared her. The name she'd promised the dragon she would know, on the other end of Rosa's rifle.*

But now all she could see was Mei's face as she took a scarlet blossom out of her hair and offered it to Rosa, laughing, saying, "Have one of your kin."

Not Blood Red, *she wanted to say.* Rose Red.

PART
FOUR

I'll take first watch," Hou Yi said, her eyes on the hare that still insisted on haunting them. They hadn't spoken since Rosa had left off her telling; the memories had bloomed leaden in her chest until she needed time away from them, and Hou Yi seemed to understand.

Rosa was exhausted—wrung dry of both energy and emotions—but she wasn't sure she could sleep with . . . that being . . . watching. Still, she nodded at Hou Yi's offer and attempted to bed down on the ground. Despite her misgivings, she dropped off almost instantly, Hou Yi standing vigil in the night and locking eyes with the nose-twitching hare who stayed just on the edge of their firelight.

And Rosa dreamed.

She dreamed she was with the people she loved.

But not Mei and Xiao Hong, not her own wife and daughter. Instead, she was with another woman, one with features that were plain but arresting. A woman, and a boy.

The boy ran up to her, exuberance painted on his face. He was about ten or twelve, his eyes bright, his limbs strong.

"Come see!" he shouted, grabbing Rosa by the hand. "Come see!"

The words were not ones she knew, but somehow she understood.

Rosa felt a smile unfold inside her, even as she kept her expression mostly stern. She let the boy grab her by the hand and followed his delighted steps as he ran. Down a set of wooden steps they flew, across a bridge of logs over a lazy swamp of water, and out into an open field. Large haystacks dotted the far end, with other shapes studding them that were too far away to make out.

"No, not there!" the boy said. He pulled Rosa away from gazing across the field. "The knot. Come see the knot!"

Rosa let him lead her. They hiked around the side of the grass, past where the haystacks stood like bulbous pincushions. Rosa took in the canvas stretched over them, the painted markers, the arrow shafts spiking out in a black forest, and somehow she had known this was what she would see here; somehow this had been her work.

But the boy pulled her past, onto rougher ground, all the way to where the land once again merged into forest. He dragged Rosa over to one of the tallest trees—a pine that spiked high and straight, its branches sparse until the very top, where it pierced the autumn blue like an arrow itself.

"There!" the boy cried. "Up there!" He jumped, pointing.

Rosa cast her eyes up. High, high on the tree's rough, sticky trunk, so high she could barely see it in the brightness, a scarlet flag fluttered merrily. The shapes gradually outlined themselves for her— the scarlet marker was tied to an arrow, protruding proudly from a broad knot high up on the tree, and just below it, striking nearly the same spot . . . a second arrow.

"I did it right," the boy promised. "All the way from the line. Not one step closer!"

And somehow, in emotions not her own, pride exploded inside Rosa, a delirious mixture of love and joy so strong it hurt. She allowed it to fill her, to straighten her spine and burst out into an unstoppable grin, and the boy beamed up at her like her approval was all he hungered for in the world.

Then something made Rosa glance up, and in

front of them was Hou Yi, with an arrow nocked but not drawn, and an expression like she had just seen a ghost.

Rosa jerked awake. She was no longer bedded down on the ground, but standing, her hand extended as if to an imaginary child. But Hou Yi still stood before her, just as she had in the dream, the red firelight from the embers fluttering across her shock and horror.

"You saw," Hou Yi said.

"I . . ." Rosa spun, groping for the rifle that was back where she had slept. From exactly the same spot where it had crouched before the sun set, the hare twitched its nose at her.

The coals reflected in its eyes, transforming them to a crimson demon's eyes. Rosa jolted back.

Hou Yi whipped around to the hare as well, stumbling to Rosa's side, her usual predator's grace off-kilter. "I looked away from it," she said, sounding more shocked than guilty. "I was watching, and I looked away . . ."

Rosa raised her voice to the animal. "Did you do this? You sent us this—dream?"

It said nothing.

"Feng Meng, wasn't it?" Rosa said more softly, when long moments had passed with no change.

94

"It was," Hou Yi answered. "Many years ago."

Rosa did not know what to say. The pride and devotion from the dream kept echoing through her—Hou Yi's emotions. Rosa recognized it: The love of a parent was so strong it had terrified her sometimes.

"I can take watch," she offered finally. "If you can rest."

"I will not be able to sleep," Hou Yi said.

Rosa didn't blame her. It seemed certain now, that this hare was involved with Feng Meng.

"I'm sorry," she said. She'd known Hou Yi's past would be exposed to her, this journey, but *this* . . . some other being stealing her memory out of her head and baring it to them both . . . this was too much. A violation, with Rosa a forced witness.

Hou Yi pressed her lips together and began gathering their things to leave, never turning wholly away from the hare.

They hiked in much the same pattern for most of the night, keeping on in the same direction, because what else could they do? And as the sun rose over the dew-covered brush, they broke out onto a bluff above the sea.

"Oh," Rosa said, and cursed. Then she cursed again so Hou Yi could understand her.

"Yes," Hou Yi said. "That seems appropriate."

At least seven or eight sunbirds dove and bathed

just out past the shallows of the ocean before them, flaming and quenching, their fiery reflections dancing across the waves and making them molten gold.

Beyond them, an island rose out of the mists, a fantastic emerald specter almost glowing in the dawn light.

"That's our destination?" Rosa said.

"It is."

"How will we . . ." Her eyes trailed to the hare, sitting unconcerned, as usual. At least maybe they'd lose the animal in the crossing, although if it had been sent by Feng Meng, it would have planned on such a thing.

"I have a way." Hou Yi touched her collar. "It is . . . I should have told you. I suspected from the first that you might reject it, and now that you have told me everything you have . . . if you decide to turn back, I understand."

It must be magic—some breed of enchanted item. "I didn't come this far with you to desert you on the doorstep," Rosa scoffed.

"As you say. But you may change your mind. Finish your story, and I shall finish mine, and we shall see."

Rosa tamped down some indignation, that Hou Yi would think she had committed to this journey, trekked all this way, confessed so much of herself, only not to see it through. Had they not faced all manner of danger together, the past two years? But she excused it as the fallout from the night, or perhaps some over-consideration for Rosa's Western views on sorcery, and let it pass.

Her story was almost complete anyway. At least as much as she was willing to tell.

"Look, Red! I brought you a present." Goldie *gave her hand a flourish, and something hard and heavy fell out of it to* thunk *upon the tabletop. "You wouldn't believe what I had to do for it. And I gave up the Crown Beryl for it, too, but I said, 'It's for my Red, it must be done.'" She placed a hand dramatically across her breast and turned her face so the broken skin on her cheekbone caught the best light.*

What? What had she done? Confusion warred with concern. Rosa reached out and picked up the object.

It lay heavy and oblong in her hand. A rifle cartridge.

"You . . . gave up the Beryl?" she said. Goldie had talked of nothing else for a month before she stole the Crown Beryl, and bragged of nothing else for a year after.

"Of course I did, stupid. Because I know how much you want to slay the dragon." She beamed at Rosa.

Slay the dragon.

Slay the dragon . . .

All she wanted was for Mei to run away with her. To hell with the grundwirgen. To hell with the kingdom—Bistherne could keep eating the king's soldiers for as long as she wanted; Rosa didn't give a damn. Someone else could stop Bistherne's rampage, someone who didn't have so much blood staining her hands already, some hero with a clear conscience who was serving the people, not still playing out revenge for a murder nearly twenty years past. Some righteous person, who hadn't sat and traded jokes with her victim and wondered if there was really any difference between them.

Goldie's face drew down into an annoyed frown. "It's enchanted, you dimwit. Stop standing there with your mouth open. I think you mean to say, 'Thank you, Goldie, you're my best friend for all eternity and nobody else but you would give up a gorgeous, perfectly cut Crown Beryl just so I can slay my stupid dragon, and I will be beholden to you forever.' It better be worth it."

"I . . ."

"Or don't say it. Whatever. I know how amazing I am." Goldie tossed her head. "Just get it done before the harvest so we get invited to all the good banquets. I have a plan for them. And you owe me big now."

Rosa closed her hand around the magic cartridge. It stayed cold as a shard of ice against her palm.

This is who you are, *it seemed to say.* No escape.

"She hadn't really given up her gemstone, had she," Hou Yi said, offering a hand to Rosa as they climbed down the steep trail to the shore.

"No," Rosa said. "I found Puss flaunting it, after I came back with Bistherne's blood on my cloak, with the whole kingdom feting me for a murder. In one night I went from being a specter people whispered about in fear to a hero of the land, and it was the worst feeling in the world."

"What did Mei say?" Hou Yi asked.

Of course Hou Yi would know to ask that. "Not much, at the time. But she pulled away from me. She'd thought I was turning away from that path. I *had* been turning away from that path." Rosa paused. "Perhaps it was smarter of her, to be skeptical I could truly change."

"But you did."

Yes, she had, but not before she had undone everything, committed the final inescapable act that had decided her fate. The only one she had failed to confess to Mei. She had no plans to voice it to Hou

Yi now, even though that last crime had been the one to fall slowly through the years, threatening to crush her and anyone she dared love.

She could not rail against a destiny she had inflicted upon herself.

Aloud she said, "After the dragon, Mei and I made a bargain. I promised that was the end for me, that I was done. And she agreed to come away with me."

"And was it the end?" Hou Yi asked.

No. But close enough. "For many years," Rosa said. "We built a life together. We had . . . so many adventures together. Later Mei had Xiao Hong, and we raised her together. Then—well. The King's Justice has a long memory. My sins caught up. I think . . . all those years, I told myself I had started again, that I had become better, but . . . there is no erasing such things, is there?"

"No," agreed Hou Yi, low and gruff.

"And having a child now—it changed everything. Mei had looked past so much, been willing to forgive far more than she should have, but when Xiao Hong found out . . . I could no longer playact that I was truly the person they loved." Her mouth tasted acrid. Or maybe it was only the remnants of the smoke from a few days before. "Even if the law had not been bearing down on us, I had no place there anymore. Not after they both knew everything."

"So you left."

"I left."

The phrase was too simple. Glossing over the weeks of horror, fear, a devastated Xiao Hong spitting Rosa's past at her through tears.

She'd thought Xiao Hong would be the one wholly good thing she did with her life. The one person she protected to the end—from everything, but especially from herself.

Pure hubris.

"There was a potion I had," Hou Yi said.

Rosa glanced over at her. They'd just dropped down onto rocky sand, and Hou Yi had set her eyes on the shoreline, to start crunching toward the white-capped waves and the diving sunbirds beyond them. Rosa scrambled to follow. Behind them, the hare hopped delicately down the rocks as if it were a mountain goat.

"An enchanted potion," Hou Yi continued. "One I had been gifted to—it doesn't matter. But powerful, and dangerous. Feng Meng overheard my wife and me speaking about it, and came to the house while I was hunting and Chang E had gone to market. He didn't even have to break in; he was such a welcome guest—but once there, he tried to steal the elixir."

Chang E. Hou Yi's wife. Hou Yi had only rarely spoken the name aloud, but Rosa remembered.

"Chang E surprised him in the act," Hou Yi continued. "There was . . . a violent struggle. She tried to keep it from him. But in the end, the only way she could do so was to drink it all down herself."

Grief saturated Hou Yi's words as the rushing of the surf filled their ears and the salt breeze their senses. Rosa tried to stretch her mind to imagine such a betrayal from her own child, but her mind blanked against the monstrousness of it.

"What did it do to her?" she asked softly.

"It gave her the powers of a god," Hou Yi answered. "We still loved each other, but she . . . drifted. I continued to get older, with the concerns of a mortal, and she drifted away from me, into a whole new world that had opened for her. One where I could not follow."

"The moon?" Rosa said.

"When she left she said she would reach it. Who knows? I could barely understand her anymore when she spoke. We had grown so far apart, so quickly, and I could not pull her back. I tried. I tried so hard. But she had become a goddess."

"And that was when . . ."

"I went mad with grief and menaced the very people I'd worked to protect, until my own grasping apprentice was able to rally the townsfolk into a mob against me. Yes, you have the right of it. They thought I died that day . . . Perhaps I did. I doubt many even recall my name now."

Rosa suspected that, like herself, Hou Yi had kept some things back, but the picture was clear enough. *Lost her wife, lost her son, and in worse ways than I.* At least Rosa's losses had stemmed from her own betrayals, with the consequences falling solely on her. She was not sure how she could have continued on without the knowledge that Mei and Xiao Hong were still comfortable and safe somewhere.

"I'm sorry you have to revisit it," she tried, inadequately. But her attempts trailed off.

Directly in front of them was the hare. Somehow, even under their watchful eyes, it had appeared between them and the still-distant surf without Rosa having seen it move. Now it crouched among dried, beached tufts of seaweed, facing them.

Rosa and Hou Yi simultaneously slowed, edging toward it. This time the hare did not move with them, but stayed in place.

Hou Yi slid to the side. The hare hopped effortlessly to keep abreast of her, blocking their way.

"What now?" Rosa said.

Hou Yi hesitated and gestured uncertainly with her bow. Rosa didn't want to take that route—the hare was clearly intelligent; it might be stalking them and filling their heads with visions, but threatening its life still seemed far out of proportion.

You've killed for less before, the little voice in the back of her head reminded.

She had. But that was why she would not, now.

"If we try to go past . . ." Rosa said. The sentence seemed too ridiculous to finish. Would the hare attack them? Even knowing it wielded some type of magic, Rosa felt the absurdity of it: such a small beast, prey and not predator, trying to hurt two large, armed human beings. But if it did move to some sort of violence . . . their weapons were ranged ones. A human intelligence in a hare's body—if it turned to aggression, what might it do?

As if she had read Rosa's mind, Hou Yi slung up her bow and pulled her hunting knife.

Rosa hadn't been carrying a knife when they'd gone after the sunbirds. She cradled her rifle cautiously. It seemed like sacrilege to consider using such a well-crafted rifle as a melee weapon, but if it meant her life, she could use it like a club.

Together, they advanced. Watchfully. Slowly.

The landscape changed.

It wasn't a sudden snap, more a jarring slide into another reality, the surrounding rocks and sand and shore swelling and bubbling until they melted into a new geography. The sky bled from a dusty blue to white, with the clouds high and even enough to make the overcast pleasant.

Only the hare remained. It hopped to the side, into the grass to their right, but Rosa had stopped watching it entirely, because behind where it had sat walked a woman and a girl.

Longing socked into Rosa so hard her body gave out, her lungs clenching and her fingers trembling on the rifle. Her knees hit the suddenly present grass without her being aware of falling.

Mei and Xiao Hong. She had not seen their faces in so long.

What devil would send her such pain?

What angel would bestow upon her the wish she dared not even voice?

It took her long moments to register anything other than shock, desperation, desire. But as they approached, she saw that they were both older. More silver than black wove through Mei's long plait now, the lines in her face carved deeper, and Xiao Hong . . . she had been a child before, only barely at the height and form of a woman. Now she had . . . grown up.

I missed it, Rosa thought, and it felt like a part of her curled away and died.

But that meant . . . if this was not a lie, it was also not a memory. This was the present. This was Mei and Xiao Hong, today, wherever they were . . . with large rucksacks? Walking staffs? Each carrying a rifle?

They must be on an extended hunting trip. Off to build some new blind, follow some new track . . . late nights bonding together, hugged close in the cold, the thrill of the journey even if they came back empty-handed.

I'm missing it all.

A hand on Rosa's shoulder. She looked up to find Hou Yi's face, creased with worry.

"Your family?" Hou Yi said, her voice gentler than Rosa had ever heard it.

Rosa couldn't manage speech, but she nodded.

Mei and Xiao Hong had come to a stop only a few paces before them. Apparently unaware of Rosa and Hou Yi, they shrugged their packs to the ground and sank down upon them. Xiao Hong drew out a waterskin, and Mei, with concentrated movements, unwrapped some gleaming shapes Rosa didn't recognize. Polished stones and carvings, cylinders that must be scroll cases . . .

"You should teach me to read," Xiao Hong said, watching her mother's hands unroll one of the scrolls. Its surface cracked slightly in her fingers, the parchment flaking at the edges.

"It's a great deal to learn," Mei said evenly.

Rosa was momentarily confused—Xiao Hong had known her letters almost since she could walk—until she saw the sure ink strokes of Hou Yi's language.

Hou Yi's language—and Mei's, from when she was a child.

"But I'd better learn, hadn't I?" Xiao Hong said. "We aren't going to be able to go back home after we find her."

Mei's pale face came up, startled. "I had not . . . thought that far."

Xiao Hong smiled slightly, and Rosa was again struck by how much she had grown.

But where are you? she thought. *Why can't you return?* Had Rosa's flight not accomplished its goal? Had her crimes overtaken not only her own life, but gutted the very two people she'd meant to save?

Mei had weighted down the edges of the scroll with the stones and carvings. She studied the writing and slowly slid an ebony rabbit and a jade monkey closer together.

Then back again. Then closer.

"What is it?" Xiao Hong asked.

"It's . . . not clear." Mei once more manipulated the carvings, and a frown formed between her eyes. Rosa wanted more than anything to reach out and touch her, to feel the warmth and strength of her. But this was all an illusion, wasn't it? Wasn't it?

"Did we get off track?" Xiao Hong raised her eyes to the white-cloaked sky. "It's hard to keep on course without the sun."

But not for Mei, Rosa knew. From the very first time Rosa had taught her to hunt, Mei had displayed the direction sense of a migrating bird, following her nose unerringly even when Rosa needed a moment to adjust her bearings.

"No, we went the way we were pointed," Mei said now. "It's the readings that have changed. They are . . . confused."

Magic. The realization startled Rosa. Mei was doing something with magic. Those items . . . they were ensorcelled, in some way.

"I see the same path we were following," Mei continued. "Only . . . I must be misreading. It seems to say she is—"

Her posture straightened suddenly, like a pointer on a scent, and she snapped her head around to look directly at Rosa.

Rosa's throat closed and her heart tore into a thousand shreds just as the landscape collapsed into a jagged puzzle before snapping back into place as sea and surf, the tang of salt once again stinging their nostrils and the clouds dissolving away.

"*No—*" Rosa cried without meaning to, reaching

out so fast she would have fallen if Hou Yi's hands had not gripped her shoulders painfully.

Where Mei and Xiao Hong had sat, only rocky sand and tumbled seaweed remained. And a hare, twitching its nose at them insolently.

"Why? Why would you show me this?" Rosa lunged, swiping out at the animal. But just as it had avoided Hou Yi's arrow without a thought, the hare took one hop straight backward, out of range of her flailing arm.

Hou Yi helped Rosa regain her feet. The hare turned and finally hopped away from them, down along the beach without a care, as if it were only out for a stroll by the waves.

Rosa took a ragged breath. "They were seeking . . ."

"Seeking you. It seems so." Hou Yi's voice was distant.

Hou Yi should not have been able to understand Mei and Xiao Hong's conversation. But just as Rosa had understood Feng Meng in the dream, the hare's magic had wrought the translation.

"Was it real?" Rosa pleaded, even though she didn't expect any answer.

"If it was, they are not far," Hou Yi said. "A week's journey north, perhaps. I know those mountains."

Had there been mountains? Silhouetted against

the horizon, perhaps, Rosa vaguely recalled. Her eyes had seen only Mei and Xiao Hong.

"But why would they be here?"

"It's obvious. Isn't it?" Rosa was no longer falling, but Hou Yi had not released her grip. Now her fingers clenched even tighter, and for the first time Rosa took notice of how stiff she sounded. It took effort to pull out of her grasp and step away.

"They're looking for you," Hou Yi said. She was gazing after the direction the hare had gone, and her face was hard. "You said they broke with you. You said they forced you to leave."

"I—" She hadn't said that, had she? Not in exactly those words. But the truth was close enough to it anyway. "It had all gone wrong," she said. Desperate defensiveness washed through her, and she wasn't even sure why. "I had to leave or they would have—the King's Men had tracked me. They would have blamed Mei if I had not run; I . . . I could have surrendered myself, but Xiao Hong told me, she told me to go . . ."

"Out of love," Hou Yi said. "I see now. To save you. How can you be so blind?"

"I'm not—what?"

"You don't *see*. They did not chase you away from *them;* they chased you from those who would do you harm. And now they seek you and *you run from them.*"

"I didn't know they were here!" Rosa's thoughts spun. "How they discovered, I don't even know—"

"If my wife and son sought me, nothing in the world could stand in my path. *Nothing.*"

Rosa was shocked into silence. Hou Yi's eyes glittered with anger, more fury than Rosa had ever seen in her.

"Go," Hou Yi said bitterly, flinging a hand toward the north. "You only imagine this prison of yours. You can have everything you want."

"I don't want . . ."

Rosa couldn't tell how everything had gotten so turned around. She was unmoored, swimming in confusion and faced with an argument that did not even make enough sense for her to counter. "I would have destroyed them," she protested. "I still—I shouldn't be near them. Not with who I am—"

"And you've made that decision?" Hou Yi almost sneered. "They feel your lack enough to trek halfway around the world to forgive you; they give their souls for the magic to find you—and you scorn them? *How dare you?*"

Rosa was suddenly, viscerally reminded of Mei, barely eighteen years old, shouting in her face. *I'm not good for you,* Rosa had said. *I don't deserve you . . .*

How dare you, Mei had demanded. *The moment I*

am free to make my own decisions, you tell me I cannot? How dare you?

She'd been truly angry. Rosa had tried to tell her, then, of her last, great crime, the only one Mei hadn't known, the only lie that had lain between them. But Mei refused to let her.

Maybe she had known, even all those years ago. She'd always been wiser about the world than Rosa had been prone to assume.

And now, once again, Mei was refusing to let Rosa protect her, refusing to live the life of less heartache Rosa had tried to gift her.

She and Xiao Hong both, so willful and stubborn and *wrong*.

"Go," Hou Yi said again, disgusted.

"I . . ." Rosa wanted to say again that she couldn't, that they didn't deserve to be saddled with her, that she didn't deserve to be part of their lives, but none of that seemed to stand up in the face of Hou Yi's argument. "You need me," she said finally, faintly.

"What are you afraid of?" Hou Yi said.

PART
FIVE

What are you afraid of?

The question burned, even as Rosa rejected it on its face. Besides, it wasn't *right,* that Rosa could just go back to the people she loved, that she would face no punishment of any consequence, that she could have Mei and Xiao Hong and they could have her when all the people she had wronged had nothing.

And she had made a commitment, here, to Hou Yi. One that had sudden gravity—Rosa had been so casual, before, about risking her life for this partnership, for what had she had left? Not that she had anything more now, nothing more than the thin potential of a sorcerer's vision. One their enemy may have had good reason for dangling before her.

Was Feng Meng using this waking dream against them? Trying to divide them, to sever the promise

Rosa had made here, the only one she hadn't yet broken?

But whether at the hare's instigation or not, the sting of Hou Yi's words punched deep. Brushing off all of Rosa's pain and sacrifice—the guilt—the consequences, both those she'd avoided and those she'd accepted, like it was *nothing*, like Rosa had *wanted* it—

"You don't understand," she said. "You saw *one thing* and you think you know, but you don't; you can't—"

"I understand enough," said Hou Yi. She retreated from Rosa, drawing herself back as though from something foul. "You run because of your own selfishness. *You* need this penance, so you force it upon *them*."

Rosa tried to form speech, but her mind wouldn't find the right words in this language. Or indeed, any words at all.

She's just angry, she promised herself desperately. *Both her wife and son betrayed and deserted her, and she thought I was the same, and it stings her that they still seek me . . .*

They still sought her. They still sought her. Her heart leapt and sang, even as it sank, leaden and unsure.

Hou Yi was right. She might be able to walk away, right now, and have everything she longed for.

What are you afraid of?

"This isn't as simple as—they wouldn't want me to," she said, with sudden relief at the truth of the realization. "They would never let me leave you now. And I—this is not—I swear to you, I thought they could be happier without me . . ."

What did it all even mean? Did they forgive her? Or only want to try?

"You were wrong," Hou Yi said.

Rosa didn't answer.

Hou Yi resumed walking down toward the water, with strides so long Rosa had to hasten to catch her.

I can't leave her now. After . . . after, she could take time to consider it all.

"You said you'd been to this island before," she called above the waves, trying to shift the conversation back. "How did you get across?"

Hou Yi let out a snort that sounded like a bitter laugh. "Not the way we will have to go this time," she said. She turned so fast Rosa almost ran into her. "Do you know what I sought, when I came here as a youth? Immortality. My own death was to be the greatest foe I would ever conquer. I would stay young, and strong, and in my prime forever."

Rosa blinked.

"The peaches of immortality grow on this island. I didn't find them, of course—they only ripen once every three thousand years. But back then, eternity was what I desired above all else."

Rosa was still trying to wrap her head around the idea of speaking of *immortality* so easily and seriously. But she also wasn't sure why Hou Yi was flinging this information at her as if she hoped the words were sharp.

"I found it." Hou Yi laughed again. It was definitely bitter. "I found it! Far later and far to the west, I did a task for a goddess and she gave me the last of the nectar she'd brewed from those same peaches, from the crop that bloomed thousands of years ago. My greatest dream, achieved! And what did it bring me? Feng Meng betrayed me for it. My wife—my wife—" Her voice broke. "Drinking it caused her to change so quickly and completely that I lost her, as surely as if she'd died. If I knew when I gained that drug that it would be such a poison—that instead of finding eternity, I would lose them both—"

Hou Yi took a few breaths to control herself.

"You couldn't have known," Rosa offered.

"But I know now," Hou Yi said. "It was what I thought I wanted, and it destroyed everything I loved. I never sought after it again, and if someone offered me the taste of immortality now, I would not only refuse it, I would flee from the offer as if it were a monster on my heels. As you flee from killing your grundwirgen. We have both tried to run from who we were. But *you*—you are also running from your family, and I find that inexcusable. Family is more important than anything."

Rosa could not agree. She thought of her mother—she might have been better off if the woman had deserted her at birth. And Xiao Hong might have been better off if Rosa had done the same.

But even if they spoke only of the family they chose . . .

"You can't—you can say that a thousand times, but it doesn't just solve everything," Rosa argued.

"It's enough," Hou Yi said.

"You're making it too clean and easy—"

"Because it *is* easy. It's the only thing in the whole cursed world that is, and you are willfully destroying it!"

Rosa bridled. "You think you understand more about family than I do? As you keep so insistently pointing out, my family didn't leave *me*."

The accusation fell between them. Rosa's breath was loud and ragged in her ears.

She shouldn't have said that. Should not have . . .

"You want so much to *accompany* me, Flower?" Hou Yi said. "You *demand* it? Well, here is how I planned to get across the channel."

She reached into her collar to draw a heavy

pendant out from under her clothes, the type some folk used to keep something precious or dangerous that they dared not store away from themselves, and pried it open to pinch out something small and brown.

"The elixir of immortality was not the only gift I ever received from a grateful god. I was a *hero*, remember? If you so want to follow me, then chew *this*. And then swim hard!"

Hou Yi flung some of the bits at Rosa's feet and thumbed the rest into her mouth. Then she ran at the waves.

Clothes, bow, woman, and all—they coalesced and spiraled in a rainbow of iridescence. Hou Yi leapt, and the transformation finished taking hold of her in the air, until only a large silver fish dove into the surf.

Rosa stood speechless.

No wonder Hou Yi had not told her.

Rosa's own righteous proclamations came back at her. *You need me. They would never let me leave you.* Her insistence to herself that she was following a friend for all the right reasons.

She bent and gathered the brown bits from among the stones and sand—some sort of dried plant or fungus, maybe.

She should have expected something like this.

Hadn't Rosa herself received just such a gift once, a bribe from an obsequious witch? What she'd done with her potion she didn't like to think about.

This one can't be a permanent transformation, though, can it? Not like the one she'd used. Wouldn't Hou Yi have warned her if it were?

But even the thought of giving up her humanity temporarily, for the brief minutes it took to reach the island—Rosa's insides writhed.

You ask too much, she thought, and then, guiltily: *She didn't ask. You volunteered.*

She'd volunteered because this was the type of friend—the type of family—she wanted to be. One who didn't betray and abandon. One who stayed stalwart in times of need.

She thought of Mei, and Goldie, and what she'd done to them both. Now Hou Yi shouted in her face on this lonely beach, telling Rosa she'd deserted her family for selfish reasons, that she'd only sacrificed because it was what *she* wanted, somehow, in some twisted dark way that was apparently the heart of Rosa's soul.

She gazed down at the small brown bits of enchantment in her callused palm.

Last chance, they seemed to say to her. *Who do you want to be?*

She felt sick.

But then she closed her eyes, clapped her palm to her mouth, and ran.

Rosa lost time between the moment she heaved in a breath and held it, the sea-foam kissing her ankles, and when she became aware of herself underwater.

Everything was color and light, a maelstrom of motion—the undertow dragging her deep, the breakers crashing her toward the shore, the currents tearing her up and down and to the side. Every sense had gone inside out, like her mind had turned slick. She could think, she could move—and in moving, she swam; she could feel herself swimming as if it happened easier than thought—but which way? Which way? How?

She struck off in the direction that seemed to counter the waves, everything rushing sound and vibration with no certainty even of up or down. She only knew she'd chosen the right way when a massive beak stabbed into the water next to her.

Rosa would have screamed if she'd had voice. The water went hot, bubbles erupting just above her where it flash-boiled. She dove, arrowing down for darkness and cold. Another shape darted past her, a fish—another fish, she corrected herself—and the massive, red-hot bird's head plunged again, this time catching the silvery shape and snapping it up out of the depths.

Had that been Hou Yi? Rosa couldn't know.

With depth came silence, and pressure, and a sort of *smell*, like wet seaweed. Rosa grasped for her sense of direction. The cold and pressure began to stall her, and she struggled back toward the surface; she felt like she was gasping even as she could not feel herself breathe.

This time a claw nearly caught her. Fire churned the water to her other side—the cursed sunbirds were everywhere—Rosa dipped and dove, pushing her slick, wriggling body until her fins ached and her skin wanted to burst along its seams. Faster, harder—how far was it? Would this ever end? Rosa was good at finding her way on land, but she could not be certain she hadn't turned around completely, or been waylaid off to the side to miss the island and be lost in the depths.

She was just beginning to believe she'd finally made it past the sunbirds when she truly stopped being able to breathe.

She wasn't even sure how she knew. It was somehow the same feeling as being on land and lacking air, only in this form she didn't even know *how* to fix it, how to take a breath, if something in the water pressing on all sides was smothering her somehow—she strove and kicked, no, not kicked, she had a *tail*, but her aquatic body was suddenly uncoordinated. A wall rose up out of the murky darkness—not a wall—mud—tree roots—

Rosa's senses were closing over and going dark. She thrashed the last few lengths, hardly aware of what she was doing. When she broke the surface, the world bifurcated with a terrible vertigo, and all she could be conscious of was being unable to breathe in *two* directions at once before some vestige of awareness let her flick herself out of the lapping water and beach herself.

The return of her humanity was surprisingly discomfiting. Her body stretched into limbs and lungs, shapes that didn't feel right for the first few moments, weighted down by the constrictions of clothes and boots and rifle.

Rosa lay on the pebbled beach and breathed. She felt like she should be coughing, but somehow, she wasn't. She groped for her rifle with sudden panic to check it over, but it was dry—as were her clothes, save where her cloak had begun picking up the dampness of the ground.

She pushed herself to sitting. The world dizzied her with its solidity.

The beach she'd landed on was on the inside of a wide lagoon. The waves here lapped quietly, mists trailing above them. Some type of lush, fantastic trees towered thickly behind her and all along the shore, their canopy stretching so far overhead that the entire lagoon felt draped in green. The air filled her newly reformed lungs with warm humidity.

She had a moment of wonderment at the climate—markedly different from the nearby coast—before she felt something else. A soft buzz against her skin, like the air was filled with a thousand tiny hummingbirds.

Magic.

The whole island was steeped in it, Hou Yi had said. And Rosa had just swum here as a . . . she should have felt more disgust. She was a grundwirgen herself now, wasn't she?

But the reflexive revulsion didn't come. She'd survived the change, everything happening too fast for her to do more than react, and here on the other side, her expected reaction only felt like a pale shadow of itself. A description of a description, as told to somebody else.

She'd tried to let it go for so long. She realized now—ashamed—that she'd only been clinging harder, convinced somehow that it was part of herself.

Rosa took a deep breath of the healing, humid air, and stood, raking the beach with her eyes for Hou Yi. The stones were small and flat and silty, gleaming in the wet like red-brown jewels, in some places clawed over by tangled cages of tree roots. Water-pebbled vines and wide leaves draped themselves over everything.

Rosa heard Hou Yi before she saw her—thrashing and coughing came from around a cluster of vegetation. Rosa had to scale a knot of stilted, moss-rich root system in order to jump down to where Hou Yi had washed ashore.

Retaking human form was giving her more trouble than it had Rosa. She had gathered herself on all fours, and kept coughing, hacking out mouthfuls of seawater.

"You're supposed to start breathing the air now," Rosa said wryly, bending to offer her a hand.

Hou Yi turned her face up with watering eyes. "You came," she croaked.

Rosa helped her up. "I came. Now let's finish this so we can go back to hurling insults at each other."

Hou Yi tried to laugh through her coughing.

Something screamed overhead.

Rosa had her rifle in her hands before she'd registered the sound. She'd heard it too often. Hou Yi, too, had straightened immediately, an arrow nocked and pointed skyward.

"This is where they're from," Hou Yi said, though

she sounded uncertain. "They may simply be . . . here, not aiming to attack."

A second cry overlapped with the first. Rosa glimpsed fire flickering through the canopy.

"They won't attack unless I tell them to," a voice said.

Hou Yi and Rosa both whipped around. A man stood only a few paces away, at the border where the narrow beach was overtaken by the jungle.

Feng Meng. Rosa recognized him both from the shape she had seen by firelight and the boy he had been in the dream, though he was much older now, his features twisted and bitter.

And he held a bow. Arrow nocked and drawn tight, the cruelly sharp head aimed directly at Hou Yi's heart.

Rosa wasn't sure why he hadn't already loosed. He'd had the moment, when she and Hou Yi were distracted by the sunbirds, but he seemed to need some sort of confrontation first—or maybe he was confident enough in his control of the birds to think he had all the time he desired. But he'd given Rosa and Hou Yi the instant they needed to focus on him, and now Hou Yi, too, had her nocked arrow pointed straight at his, and Rosa's sights cradled a fatal shot.

Rosa's heart thumped, her hands slick against

the rifle stock. A man in her sights, for the first time in many years. A human form in her sights for the first time ever.

She stood very still, her stance unwavering. The birds wheeled overhead and screamed.

"You brought a friend," sneered Feng Meng. "Is she your new lover? Will you destroy and abandon her, too?"

Hou Yi did not seem able to respond.

Rosa called out, "We've come to stop you. You're sending the sunbirds to kill and terrorize. We cannot let you continue."

"I'm only following in the footsteps of my mentor," Feng Meng said. "*You* showed me how to respond to grief, dear teacher. I'm only doing as you taught me."

"I have no wish for you to repeat my worst mistakes," Hou Yi said, low and shaking. It cut Rosa to hear.

"And it gives me no pleasure to be you," Feng Meng shot back. "But you hollowed me out and made me into this shape, and whatever I poured into the emptiness, it has still hungered only for your *approval*."

"Mine?" Hou Yi said faintly.

"I despise myself," Feng Meng said. "I despise this thing you made me into."

Rosa might have tried to allow for sympathy, but

she had not spent a lifetime trying to own her past in order to let someone dodge responsibility in front of her. "Your life is your own," she cut in. "You cannot blame some imagined slights by Hou Yi for the acts you commit now."

"Ha!" Feng Meng said. "I'm the villain in your little opera then, am I?"

Hou Yi had fallen silent again—Rosa didn't blame her; she could not have faced her own child this way.

Rosa spoke for her. "I know your story. Hou Yi is not without failings, but nor are you. If you want to make an accounting of her wrongs, then do so, but you stole from her and tried to murder her. You betrayed her and were the reason her wife was driven away. And now you kill innocent people for your revenge, and we are here to stop you."

To Rosa's surprise, instead of arguing back, Feng Meng's face crumpled in grief, and tears sprang to his eyes.

"Is this what you tell people?" he said to Hou Yi. "Is this how you remember it?"

"I . . ." Hou Yi faltered. "I'm not . . . it's what happened."

"Which parts do you deny?" Rosa challenged him.

"None," he answered slowly. "None . . ."

He took a shuddering breath. The sunbirds shrieked overhead. Feng Meng did not release his hold on his bow, but he raised his head and let out a piercing whistle.

"I've dispersed them," he spat, the angry mask back in place. "If you think so greatly of yourself and so poorly of me, then kill me now and bury the truth of yourself with me."

"What truth?" Hou Yi said.

"What truth!" Feng Meng cast a disbelieving glance at Rosa before turning back to Hou Yi. "Did you tell your new lover about your *obsession* with immortality? Tell her. Tell her! It consumed and defined your every moment. There was no room in your heart for friendship, for affection—even your great 'heroics' were only a means to draw the gods' attention to yourself. And as for me—as for *me*—"

His voice broke. His hands had begun to shake on the bow, either from emotion or fatigue.

"The only reason you taught me was so your own vaunted skills would live on," he accused Hou Yi. "I was your *legacy*, your sad substitute for your own immortality. Until you got your hands on the real thing . . . and when you did, you were just going to go, you were going to leave, you and she but nobody else—I heard you say so! You told me I was like your son, and you were going to leave me behind like so much rotten meat . . ."

His shouts had deflated and flattened until they

were sobbing pleas. But he drew his bowstring tighter with trembling fingers as if to give lie to the pain.

"I . . ." Hou Yi's voice was a whisper. "There was only enough for two."

Rosa's sights swayed in her vision. Hou Yi had . . . and she told *Rosa* she was deserting her child? The hare had shown them both the truth of that parental love, so strong Rosa had felt it thrumming through her . . . how could Hou Yi turn her back? How could she even conceive of it?

I would never trade Xiao Hong for a thousand eternities, she thought. But then—what reason did she have for leaving Xiao Hong now?

The vicious truth of it sliced her to the core.

"You thought I wanted to steal the bottle to gain godhood for myself," Feng Meng went on. "I only wanted to dash it on the ground. I should have known when *you* lost your chance at living forever, you would try to take the rest of us with you."

"I was taken by madness when I lost Chang E," Hou Yi said. "I did . . . I regret so many things . . ."

"When you lost—ha! You rampaged because you lost your precious elixir. And it wasn't madness you suffered; it was *arrogance.*"

Hou Yi did not speak for a long moment. Then she slowly released the tension on her bow and lowered it. "Perhaps you're right. I don't know any-more."

"Well, *I do*," Feng Meng said, and shot her.

It was so fast. His fingers slipped off the string and the bow bounced against the suddenly released tension and an arrow flew straight for Hou Yi, who still had her own bow lowered. She'd started to raise it, fast, so fast, as if she could shoot the arrow out of the air, but then the stone head slugged into her ribs and her body lost all coordination, her limbs going heavy and stiff like a wooden doll's.

Rosa squeezed the trigger.

She could not miss. She was too close; she was too good a shot; her sights were aligned. But at the last instant something made her pull the shot. Her finger dragged against the stock, her palm jerking upward.

Feng Meng staggered. His bow dropped and he nearly lost hold of it, juggling it from fingers that no longer closed, his other hand groping at his bleeding shoulder. Hurling curses at both Rosa and Hou Yi, he turned and fled, crashing into the tropi-cal brush.

Rosa swung down her rifle and dashed to Hou Yi's side. She ducked under an arm and got a hand around the other woman's shoulders. "How bad is it? Sit down—"

"No—we have to—" Hou Yi's breath tripped over itself, constricting into a bloody cough.

"Stop trying to talk," Rosa said. "We're not going after anyone. You're going to die if we don't—"

Hou Yi grabbed at Rosa's cloak, her hand fisting in the crimson material. "He might be right about me," she said thickly. "I don't . . . I don't know. He might be."

Rosa didn't know either. She could offer no comfort. Hou Yi might have been the woman she feared she was.

After all, a judgmental thought prodded, *what kind of woman would chase magic and leave her son behind?*

And, close on the heels of that: *The same type of woman who would flee her own daughter?*

Mei should have stayed away in shame. And Hou Yi's wife . . . Hou Yi must fear she was not blameless in Chang E's departure either. It might even be so—Rosa's mind could not stretch to grasp all the emotional truths Feng Meng had revealed here.

Hou Yi swayed, collapsing. Rosa shoved aside the threatening tangle of obligation and guilt, wrestling Hou Yi over to sink down on a rock. The arrow shaft protruded sickeningly, somehow as massive as a polearm, both their clothes already sopped with blood.

Rosa tore off her muffler and bunched it around the wound. Red stained red.

"The arrowhead," Hou Yi got out. "Has to be pulled . . ."

"Bullets you don't—" started Rosa.

"Arrows you do."

It would not have been what Rosa expected, being told to tear out the arrowhead—would that not damage a body more? But she was no surgeon. She only knew what little she did about gunshot wounds because of so frequently being the cause of them.

She followed Hou Yi's stilted instructions, sliding her fingers down the slick shaft, into her friend's flesh, dark and hot and drenching. Her friend; her friend with a past full of sins as dark as Rosa's, her friend who had wanted to desert her son, her friend whose son had tried to kill her twice over. Rosa's fingers found the hard outline of the stone arrowhead and tried to pinch at the edges. Hou Yi grunted and jerked.

Rosa froze, then tried again, more slowly, but her grasp was too slippery. By the time the arrowhead slid free with her hand, as long as her first finger and thin and sharp like a blade, Hou Yi had clenched Rosa's other wrist so hard she'd left bruises. She had gone white and sweating, her skin clammy and too cold.

Rosa tried to press the wound closed, filling it with her muffler and then her cloak and binding the fabric as tightly around Hou Yi's chest as she could. The makeshift bandages sagged, heavy with blood.

"Fitting . . ." Hou Yi murmured wetly. "This death. It is fitting . . ."

To be killed by her own son. Even with the guilt Hou Yi carried . . . Rosa could not agree.

"He is so angry." Tears had begun sliding from the corners of Hou Yi's eyes, and Rosa was certain they were as much from grief as pain. "So angry at me. I never knew . . ."

Love, even more than hate, could always sharpen anger to the keenest of points. Rosa again saw Xiao Hong screaming at her, accusing her of sacrificing Mei to save her own skin.

It had never been about saving herself. She had no hope of that. But when it came to saving Xiao Hong's image of her—then, then she had indeed been a coward. Such a coward.

Why had they not let her stay one? Why had they insisted on chasing?

"I can't judge," she said to Hou Yi. They were the most comforting words she knew how to say.

Hou Yi's hand came up to grip one of Rosa's, slipping against her skin and leaving sticky tracks behind. "Flower. Please. Before I die . . . I want to tell him . . ."

Rosa leaned forward, bringing her ear closer to Hou Yi's lips.

"I want to ask his forgiveness," she whispered. "My son. Please. Help me."

It was a last request; they both knew it. Rosa could not deny her. The two women struggled together to pull Hou Yi's body upright until she leaned heavily against Rosa's shoulder, her arm slung across, her boots dragging in a semblance of walking.

They took one lurching step and almost fell, then another, their progress elongated agonizingly minute after minute. *She will not last to find him,* Rosa thought, but she said nothing.

"Make me a promise," Hou Yi gasped against her. Blood bubbled at the side of her mouth. "Find your Mei. Find them both, and see . . ."

The island had begun to shift into twilight, even more so under the soaring trees and away from the clearing provided by the lagoon. Rosa concentrated on finding their feet in the dimness, trying to avoid being tripped by the dense undergrowth.

"Promise me, Flower," said Hou Yi.

"I don't—I don't know if I can." Rosa's eyes burned and blurred.

"They want . . . to forgive you . . ."

"You asked what I was afraid of." Rosa kicked through a tangle of vines and roots. "They know . . . they know all of me, now. They know what I am. I don't want to see that in their eyes when they look at me." Her voice cracked. "I want to remember them loving me, not—it's too hard. You're right. I am a coward."

Hou Yi was silent for so long that her harsh breathing in Rosa's ear and the stumbling shuffle of her feet along with Rosa's were the only assurance she hadn't bled her life onto the forest floor. Rosa's troubles must have become pitiful to Hou Yi, such a weak excuse for tragedy. The other woman had nearly accused her of such on the beach, and now . . . Rosa's family still chased her, as broken as such an act was, while Hou Yi's son shredded her heart. And Hou Yi's wife long gone, the so-called goddess in the moon.

Perhaps it had always been a metaphor for how lost Chang E had become to her. How irreversible the cost.

But Hou Yi didn't know the worst secrets Rosa still carried. The past betrayals that tainted every possible future with Mei and Xiao Hong, now that they knew. The truth of what kind of woman she was.

"Tell me," Hou Yi whispered in her ear then, and Rosa wondered if the strange magic of this island had exposed her thoughts.

More likely they were too similar for Hou Yi not to have understood after all. To have seen the emptiness that was missing from her story.

"Please," Hou Yi said, the words faint, hitching between breaths. "Tell me the rest. Let a dying woman know . . . she is not alone . . . in the dark."

She wasn't speaking of the deepening night.

Rosa cleared her throat.

"I told you, I can't judge. And . . . I can't. My hands were stained already, but when I . . . I betrayed Mei . . ."

And Goldie. It was so strange, how she could still feel guilt about that. What she had done to the woman who had wanted to steal her life but whom Rosa would always feel she owed, forever, with no amount of logic able to dissuade it.

Until Hou Yi, she'd destroyed everyone she'd sworn loyalty to.

Rosa tore apart her bed for the seventh time. Clothes and shoes and knickknacks scattered themselves from one end of the room to the other.

She didn't care. She wasn't taking them. She only wanted her other cloak, and she couldn't find it.

And she had to find it, and find it quickly, because Goldie wasn't here right now and Rosa just wanted to leave, wanted to disappear without fighting or shouting or guilt or explanations. She wanted to go like a coward in the night, away from this friendship that lay around her neck like a lead weight and into the arms of the woman who made her light and free.

"What on earth are you looking for?"

Rosa turned. Puss stood in the doorway, on his hind legs in a way that had always struck her as entirely unnatural for a cat. His boots only made it worse—his legs always looked like they bent the wrong way in them.

"I can't find my other cloak," Rosa said, with biting dignity. "Have you seen it?"

"Oh, I have, in fact." He licked a front paw in apparent unconcern and didn't continue.

Rosa picked up her rifle. No more than that.

Puss laid his ears back and squinted his eyes at her, as if to scorn her attempt at intimidation. "You pathetic humans. Goldie took your cloak, if you must know. Whatever catfight you two are in the middle of, I want no part of it." He chortled his hitching hiss of a laugh. "Catfight! The irony."

Rosa ignored him. She retrieved her hunting pack from where she'd let it fall behind the bed and slung it over one shoulder, then pushed past Puss out of the room, not caring if she knocked him over. Cats always landed on their feet.

"She'd gone . . . to bloody you . . ." Hou Yi said, her voice threaded with weakness.

Shocking, that Hou Yi could see it all so quickly. It had taken Rosa herself far too long to realize, to come to the right conclusion and dash after. How long had Goldie known of Rosa's plans? When had she contrived to keep Rosa by her side by sullying her in the eyes of her lover? Goldie had planned to slay the Beast in Rosa's cloak and then . . . what? Leave the bloody cloak for Mei to find? Or maybe fling a scrap of it at the scene and then alert the King's Men, determined that if her best friend were to desert her, Rosa's life would be forfeit as punishment?

"Tell me," murmured Hou Yi, heavy against Rosa's shoulder.

"I raced after her." Rosa forced herself on. "To the Beast's castle. Mei was not there; she had already fled, to meet me at our rendezvous, where I was supposed to be."

There had only been darkness, a raging monster of a man, and a girl with gold curls and a red cloak who danced before him, twirling a repeater and taunting.

Rosa brought up her rifle, shouting, her sights wavering between them.

"You aren't going to shoot me, Red!" Goldie called,

flinging her own pistol back and forth with no regard for the proper handling of a weapon. "You need me. I saved you! We need each other!"

"Shoot her!" the Beast demanded in a roar. "Shoot her, shoot her!"

But Rosa couldn't.

She couldn't. She flashed on Mei begging her to promise, insisting that "these things are complicated"—that Rosa must not kill the Beast because Mei did love him, despite all—and she finally understood.

These things were complicated. She knew without trying that she would never be able to kill Goldie, no matter what, even if the woman turned her pistol on Rosa herself. Just as Mei could not punish the Beast for what he had done to her.

Her rifle dropped. Goldie laughed triumphantly, and the Beast wailed and roared. And Rosa felt the bulge in the pocket of her hunting pack, the one she'd kept but never thought of using, the witch's ugly potion that she'd scorned for years and years but couldn't bring herself to discard because it was, after all, a weapon. Hardly knowing what she was doing, she drew it out and flung.

The gray-green powder hit her closest friend in a cloud, drifting down over yellow hair and stolen red cloak.

Goldie's laughing, mocking triumph twisted into shock and hurt. Her huge blue eyes went to Rosa asking why and how could you *almost too fast to see*, before her features began to contort and shrink away. Her skin went brown and bumpy and her limbs dwindled and curled into themselves and her clothes seared themselves to brittle dust.

In seconds, all that was left of Goldie was a largish, warty toad. It gazed up at Rosa, and she fancied she saw such hurt in those animal eyes, yellow eyes the same color as Goldie's hair.

It croaked at her, and fled.

The Beast gave a cry and prostrated himself at Rosa's feet, promising her the world, babbling in gratitude. And Rosa . . .

She gazed down at him and thought of Mei.

She gazed down at him, and thought of Mei, and thought of how Mei had made her promise not to kill him, how she had promised not to kill anyone anymore, that they would flee together and build new lives.

She gazed down at him, and remembered that he was cursed, that the reason he had stolen Mei's life was that he needed the love of another, and that he was engineering his release by keeping a girl shut up with him forever with no other company until she loved him back, and how it had almost worked.

She thought of the next girl, and the next, and for

the last time, she raised her rifle and squeezed her finger back.

It was so easy.

"It was the only lie between us," Rosa said. "The only thing I never told her. Maybe she suspected. I have wondered. Certainly she must have later . . ."

When Mei had been arrested for the crime. The crushing weight of Rosa's nightmare becoming fact. It had paralyzed her.

"I think I am . . . a broken person," she confessed to Hou Yi. "Too much of my being has been the hunt. Killing. Even the years with Mei and Xiao Hong . . . I think I was only pretending."

"Not true," Hou Yi whispered.

"It is true. I kept trophies; did I say?" She knew she had not said. "Not because I was proud. At least not most of them. But because it was all I had. For so many years. I couldn't let go."

"I mean . . . it is not true . . . you pretending," Hou Yi managed. "The reality is . . . you . . . you have both the bad and good. You always . . . oversimplify, Flower."

And then she started to laugh, though it quickly aborted into a hacking cough.

"I'm not—!" It was hard to argue with someone

who was dying against her shoulder while *mocking her.* "Knowing what I am—I'm not oversimplifying. Stop laughing!"

"You want to be . . . so tragic a figure," Hou Yi wheezed. "Don't worry, I agree you have done . . . very bad things . . . I would have killed you myself, if we had met back when I was the hero and you were the villain. But you think too much of yourself. Now we are just two old women." The momentary teasing strength faded to sadness. "Old women who have hurt their children."

Old women who have hurt their children.

The words rang in Rosa's head as they limped along in silence, their legs and feet dragging and crashing through the brush. It was almost too dark to see, now. Fortunately Feng Meng's flight was easy to follow; he'd been badly injured enough himself to crash a broken path through the undergrowth.

Old women who have hurt their children.

On some level Rosa had always seen her flight as a type of consequence. She had run from the punishment the law would have meted out to her— imprisonment, or more likely execution. Didn't she merit whatever lonely emptiness filled her life now?

She'd never thought of it as another in her long string of wrongs, this time against Mei and Xiao Hong. She'd never thought of it as an act that *hurt them.* She'd regretted every toxic part of herself and her past with vicious self-loathing, but leaving had always seemed the proper choice, the choice that spared them, and the way it had torn Rosa to the core had only added to the righteousness of it.

Now she saw it for what it was: only a clumsy, flawed decision, like so many others along the twisting path that had brought her here.

She'd spoken truly to Hou Yi a moment ago, even more truly than she'd known. She was a coward. She didn't want to face her family not because deserting them was somehow the moral choice, but because she didn't want to own up to the fact that she had hurt them so badly.

It had been so much *easier,* running. Running, and telling herself she'd done what was best.

Hou Yi stumbled and dragged against her. Rosa tightened her grip, keeping them upright by the force of panic alone.

"Hey!" Rosa said, louder and sharper than she intended. "I'll make a deal with you. I'll go find my family"—her heart beat faster—"if you find yours. Do you hear me? You have to live. If I have to . . ." If she had to face the terrifying task of rebuilding her relationship with Mei and Xiao Hong, if she had to face the chance that she might fail—"Do you hear me? We do this together."

"I . . . do not think . . ." Hou Yi's voice was so weak now Rosa could barely hear her, even with her lips so close to Rosa's ear. "I think my son has already . . . rejected . . . your plan for me . . ."

Rosa tried to bring up an appropriately caustic response to that sort of humor, but before she could, they stumbled out into a clearing, one so large that the starlit night stretched wide above them.

The first thing Rosa noticed was the full moon, impossibly huge, a giant white pearl suspended in a sky that was now velvet black. The woods surrounded them in dark shades of silver, as if the trees had themselves been carved from moonlight.

A broad slope of smooth rock formed the floor of the clearing, with a spring bubbling into a clear pool in the middle, and behind the pool, its roots sprawling wide and gnarled, a single ancient tree spread its branches over the scene. It looked like it might fill the place with a heady perfume at another time, but now its limbs were heavy only with tight, clustered buds. And at the end of a long, black smear, collapsed by the water, lay the dying form of Feng Meng.

Rosa felt a stab of guilt and grief. *I did that. I've killed him.*

Feng Meng might not be blameless. But if he deserved to die . . . well, she and Hou Yi's souls were just as rancid.

There was no justice here, only death.

Hou Yi lunged forward, and Rosa helped her stagger the last short distance, until they fell against the tree at the edge of the pool. Hou Yi lay half across Rosa, a dead weight.

Feng Meng's eyelids fluttered. "I thought I wanted to see you die," he bit out. "But perhaps it's best if you see me die first. That's what you wanted, isn't it? To watch me die, and then live on forever."

Hou Yi tried to lift a hand toward him, but it dropped back to the ground. "I never wanted that," she said. "I never . . . I was so shortsighted. You were right; I saw only my own desires. I didn't—I didn't think."

"Yes," Feng Meng said. "You never thought of me. No matter how much I worked to please you."

"I'm sorry," Hou Yi pleaded. "I'm sorry. My son. I failed you."

Feng Meng coughed and spit blood into the crystalline water, and when he spoke, it was not to forgive.

"Ha. The easy path. You say this and then escape from this life—you could never love in a way that did not suit you; you don't have the capacity. It's work you would never do, and I won't release you to death thinking you made up for a lifetime in one instant—"

Something pawed at Rosa's hip.

She twisted to look around, and jerked back against the tree, trapped by Hou Yi's body. The hare. The hare had followed them here somehow.

Rosa wanted to crawl out of her skin.

The hare pawed her again, regarding her with solemn eyes, and then sat back on its haunches to stare upward. Rosa slowly tracked its gaze. The full moon shone through the branches of the tree above them, a round disc of polished silver-white with black leaves laid across it like cut-out paper. The moon was low, and the branch crossing it hung heavy in the foreground, its thick bundles of buds close enough for Rosa to reach out and touch.

The moon . . .

Something inconceivable tickled at Rosa, the intersection of magic and gods and demons, here on this island that defined its own tilted reality.

The hare raised up on its hind legs, pawing at the air, and then back down. A drift of clouds crossed the moon, and at the moment they passed the moonlight seemed to grow brighter, the leaves gleaming in the beam like a metal sculpture. And there hanging from the tree branch—

Rosa blinked. Even in the dark, she would have sworn the thing had not been there a moment ago, as if it had grown from one of the curled buds in the space of one blink itself: a small, flat fruit, squat and round like a flower, or the shape of an apple compressed top to bottom.

Do you know what I sought? The peaches of immortality, Hou Yi had said, so angrily . . . a fruit that only ripened once every three thousand years.

But Chang E, Hou Yi's wife—with the powers of a goddess—*When she left she said she would reach the moon. Who knows?*

The moonlight shone through the branches, making the squat little fruit glow. What did gods do, if not the impossible?

The hare batted at the air again. The moon seemed to shimmer down at them like it was winking, and for a moment Rosa was certain she saw the hare's shape reflected in its surface.

Could it be that Rosa's wife wasn't the only one who followed?

Hou Yi and Feng Meng were still spilling their dying repartee, words falling discordant and bloodied into the pool between them. The hare turned back to Rosa and twitched its ears.

"I don't understand," Rosa said to it, even though she thought she did. *Find your family,* she'd told Hou Yi. She hadn't known she'd spoken of something possible.

Magic. Gods. One last chance to take the hard

path, the right path. And no one had more reason to ask that of these two than Chang E.

In the moonlight, in this quiet, fantastic clearing, anything seemed imaginable.

Rosa reached out her hand and tugged at the squat little peach. It took a hard twist to break it awkwardly off into her hand, and she worried she'd bruised it—the flesh was soft and ripe, full to bursting with its juices. It was small enough to fit within her palm, the skin pale and velvety soft.

She glanced back once more at the moon, and somehow it seemed to nod.

"Stop," she said. Hou Yi's and Feng Meng's hopeless, fractious last words scattered into silence.

Rosa held out the peach.

For a moment the silence was as heavy as death.

Then Hou Yi tried to push her hand away, too weakly. "No . . . no, what is this? I told you, it ruined me, and you would tempt me now? Why? . . . How?"

"You could do the work," Rosa said. "You could promise. If he will let you try." She extended the fruit to Feng Meng.

He gazed blankly at her from the ground, uncomprehending, his face half in the bloodied spring.

"Are you determined to die here and make your mother watch?" Rosa asked quietly.

"Give it to him instead," Hou Yi said. "I can't make up . . . the first time . . . but let him have a second chance. I beg you, Flower."

"There's enough for two," Rosa said. She dug her fingers into the tiny fruit's flesh and twisted it apart.

Feng Meng took his in limp fingers and did not bring it to his lips. Rosa had to fold Hou Yi's hand around hers, next to her mouth, only the smallest movement away from living forever.

An eternity of working to earn back the trust and love of her family. The prospect dizzied Rosa just to contemplate.

The hare hopped forward and stood with one paw braced on Rosa's thigh, watching, the moonlight gleaming against its fur.

Hou Yi found Feng Meng's eyes one more time, and she would have spoken too softly to hear if not for the stillness of the clearing. "I won't . . . unless you ask it," she said. "If you live, or no, I won't unless you want me to. If you do . . . I want to try to make up for the lifetime . . . even if it takes many more. I promise . . ."

Feng Meng blinked, and suddenly, behind the anger, Rosa glimpsed such a depth of neglected pain, the face of the ten-year-old boy who had been so proud to show off his archery skills and then so broken at being discarded.

Barely perceptibly, he nodded.

Hou Yi struggled to turn and shift back to Rosa. The hand that did not hold the fruit fisted in Rosa's clothing. "You promise me, too. Together. You said."

"I promise," Rosa said, and she was crying.

Hou Yi slipped the small slice of impossible peach into her mouth.

The moonlight seemed to grow brighter, and brighter, until it overwhelmed every sense, until the trees were silhouetted black on white instead of silver in the darkness. Rosa could not have sworn to what came next—sight and sound and feeling were all somehow both intensified and absent. Hou Yi's weight was gone from her, but Rosa didn't feel her own weight either, so that seemed to mean very little.

But then Rosa saw two people standing—Hou Yi and Feng Meng, their forms indistinct but somehow clear, standing at a careful distance from each other, considering, taking the first step toward bridging the emptiness between them. And when she turned her head to the side, Rosa saw the hare, the moonlight emanating so brightly it seemed the animal stood in its very source, and next to the hare, a woman, a woman Rosa had seen in a dream whose face was plain but arresting, a woman who carried herself like a god and gazed at Hou Yi and Feng Meng with both sadness and love.

Some sort of emotion welled within Rosa, flowing out with her tears like an unchecked mountain spring—not gladness, exactly, and not unlike a heart-stopping fear, but also something very much like hope.

Then Rosa turned to her other side, and somehow she saw—still far away but hiking closer and closer, coming straight as one of Hou Yi's arrows toward the very spot where Rosa stood—she saw Mei and Xiao Hong.

And even as Hou Yi and Feng Meng and Chang E and the magical hare burst into transcendence and were gone, Mei and Xiao Hong became ever more real and solid, and then Mei looked up and locked eyes with Rosa and stopped dead before beginning to run. And in Rosa's ear she heard the whisper of Hou Yi's voice: "Promise. Together."

Rosa only had the tail end of a single lifetime, but she thought it might be just enough.

ACKNOWLEDGMENTS

Writing and publishing are so very far from being an island. On this one, I owe many, many thanks to my editor, Diana Gill, who made this book a reality and put her faith in it from start to finish. She is joined by her colleague Kristin Temple, assistant Robert Davis, the tireless team at Tordotcom Publishing—Irene Gallo, Mordicai Knode, Ruoxi Chen, and Christine Folzer—my publicist, Lauren Anesta; my cover artist, Victo Ngai; and everybody else at all levels of editing and production. A particularly heartfelt thanks to Ruoxi Chen for stepping in on this book under difficult circumstances during the pandemic and taking the wheel as smoothly as humanly possible. I am also extremely grateful, as always, to my agent, Russell Galen, and my film agent, Angela Cheng Caplan, who are my champions across every aspect of my career.

My first readers on this book were Rob Livermore, Effie Seiberg, Maddox Hahn, Elaine Aliment, and Jesse Sutanto; their time and perspective were invaluable. And the very first person who gave me any feedback was, as always, my sister, who is a constant in my writing life. I have no idea what I would do without her—probably wallow in despair.

A big shout-out to my uncle for helping me out with a language question!

Finally, a very, very special thanks goes out to Ana Grilo and Thea James of The Book Smugglers, who published the first stories in this universe, and without whose encouragement and support this novella would never have been written.

Many other people are of continual, invaluable help to me in both my writing and real life. I wish I could mention them all. To all of my communities—and on this one, in particular my queer, BIPOC, and feminist communities—thank you.